Supreme

"AS LONG AS YOU'RE HERE, I'LL PROTECT YOU," RYDER TOLD HER FIRMLY.

"I won't let any of those thugs touch you." He looked around the tent where Cally was being held prisoner—it was in shambles. "Did they hurt you?"

"No, I'm all right." Cally's voice trembled uncertainly. "I . . . I just wish they'd kill me and get it over with. I'm tired of being scared!" Her breath caught in a sob and her eyes filled with tears.

Ryder lifted his hands hesitantly, unsure of what to do. "It's going to be all right. I won't let anything happen to you." He tilted her face up to his. The look she gave him was one of fear, need, trust. Ryder felt his control slipping away. He lowered his head to brush a kiss across her lips. "I promise you, Cally, I'm going to get you out of here if it's the last thing I do."

CANDLELIGHT SUPREMES

PRISONER IN HIS ARMS

Dallas Hamlin

A CANDLELIGHT SUPREME

Published by
Dell Publishing Co., Inc.
1 Dag Hammarskjold Plaza
New York, New York 10017

ISBN: 0-440-17042-7

Printed in the United States of America

March 1987

10 9 8 7 6 5 4 3 2 1

WFH

To Our Readers:

We are pleased and excited by your overwhelmingly positive response to our Candlelight Supremes. Unlike all the other series, the Supremes are filled with more passion, adventure, and intrigue, and are obviously the stories you like best.

In months to come we will continue to publish books by many of your favorite authors as well as the very finest work from new authors of romantic fiction. As always, we are striving to present unique, absorbing love stories —the very best love has to offer.

Breathtaking and unforgettable, Supremes follow in the great romantic tradition you've come to expect *only* from Candlelight Romances.

Your suggestions and comments are always welcome. Please let us hear from you.

Sincerely,

The Editors
Candlelight Romances
1 Dag Hammarskjold Plaza
New York, New York 10017

PRISONER IN
HIS ARMS

CHAPTER ONE

From the moment he saw her, Ryder knew she was going to mean trouble.

He was resting in his tent, avoiding the midday heat, when he heard the truck returning. The shouts that greeted its arrival were unintelligible but excited.

Cursing under his breath, he pulled himself to his feet. It was probably nothing more than someone having shot something for dinner. Fresh meat was always a cause for some excitement. But he needed to know for sure.

He left his khaki shirt unbuttoned but he reached over to pick up his hat, shoving it on over thick black hair, a habit he'd picked up years ago. The Central American sun could be merciless and he had no intention of courting heatstroke.

His dark blue eyes narrowed against the bright afternoon sun. An old army transport truck was pulled into the center of the rude circle of huts and tents, the back of it surrounded by a crowd of laughing, gesturing men. It had to be something more than a cow pilfered from some poor farmer's yard. His muscles tensed as he strode across the clearing. He hoped it wasn't one of General Juarista's men. They had brought in a lieutenant six months ago and it still turned Ryder's stomach to think of the poor bastard's condition when he got to camp. Death had been a merciful relief.

He shoved his way through the men, ruthlessly using his size to force a path. Before he got to the back of the truck, the returning guerrillas had cleared an area in front of it and hauled out their booty. Ryder got only a glimpse of fair hair before the prisoner was shoved to the ground and out of sight.

A sudden urgency gripped him and he thrust himself quickly into the front of the group. He felt as if he had received a fierce kick in the gut when he finally got a good look at the prisoner.

The hair was fair all right. A bright golden shade of blond that seemed to catch and reflect the brilliant sunshine around them. As the captive knelt on the hard dirt, the fall of hair dragged almost to the ground around her. A woman. No, hardly more than a girl, he decided as she raised her face and looked straight at him.

Ryder was oblivious to the babble of words around him as he looked at the girl. The incredible hair framed features that were piquantly pretty. A broad forehead and narrow chin gave her face a pixie shape that was reinforced by the faint tilt to her gray eyes. Eyes that were just now filled with fear. Fear but not panic, he realized. There was awareness in those eyes, not the blank wall of panic.

She raised her rope-bound wrists to brush the hair back from her face and Ryder was surprised by the rush of anger that swept over him when he saw that the coarse rope had cut into her pale skin and the fiber was now stained with the dark tint of blood. Bruises were forming on the pale skin of her upper arms, left bare by the sleeveless top she wore.

Damn! When Tomás had suggested kidnapping a wealthy American, Ryder had thought he had managed to talk him out of it but there was no other reasonable explanation for this blond girl's presence. Her eyes, which had widened slightly when she saw him, now shifted to skim over the men he stood among. He expected contempt when she saw he was an accepted member of the group but, instead, the blazing hope in her eyes faded to be replaced by returning fear, and she dropped her eyes back to the hard dirt beneath her.

"Ay, Rico, you see what I have done?" Ryder shifted his eyes away from the prisoner to the man who swaggered into the center of the small clearing to stand next to the girl. He had never liked Tomás Moreno but, at that moment, he decided that he hated the cocky little bastard. Tomás was the leader of this mixed bag of terrorists and criminals. Officially, they called themselves a liberation army and spoke grandly of freeing the country from the oppressive rule of the government. There might even have been a few among them who believed this line of drivel.

In reality, they were nothing more than a bunch of society's outcasts—murderers, thieves, and rapists—men who could claim no home, no family. Men with nothing to lose and a natural leaning toward violence. The "Freedom Army" was universally hated and feared by their countrymen. Time and again, the government had set out to eradicate them but the government had few men and even fewer who knew the hills and jungles as Tomás and his men did. So far, the points had been all on Tomás's side.

Ryder had joined the ragtag band close to a year ago. He'd brought with him information on troop movements that had allowed Tomás to avoid several confrontations with the government and a reputation for being a man with no loyalties. His knowledge of jungle warfare was unmatched by any of Tomás's men and had proved valuable on more than one occasion. With all that, it had still taken him months to get Tomás to trust him. And now, he might have to risk it all for the girl who knelt in the dirt before him.

Ryder forced a half-smile to his lips, resisting the urge to drive his fist into the other man's mouth and knock out the one front tooth that remained there. He answered the man in the same language he had spoken in, his tongue curling over the words as if he were a native.

"I see that you have brought a child to our camp but I fail to see the reason why."

Tomás grinned widely, exposing numerous gaps in his yellow teeth. "Ay, Rico, you still do not understand my brilliance." He glanced around as if seeking some agreement from the other men and they obliged him by nodding. "This is not a child. She is a young woman, Rico. Has it been so long since you spent time with a woman that you have forgotten what one looks like?"

This brought a murmur of amusement from his audience and, encouraged by this, Tomás reached down to wind a grimy hand in the shining fall of hair, drawing her head back until her neck was arched at a painful angle. He bent and hooked the fingers of his other hand in the neck of her blouse and, with easy strength, he ripped the garment down the front, exposing an expanse of white skin banded only by the fragile lace of her bra. The peach fabric did little to conceal the firm thrust of her breasts and Ryder could feel the sudden change in the atmosphere around him. Lust rose in almost visible waves.

The girl did not cry out but he could see the shudder that ran over her slender frame.

His voice carried none of the tension he felt. "You are right, Tomás. She is not a child but I still see no reason for her to be here."

It was a moment before Tomás raised his eyes from the girl he held helpless beneath him. There was a gleam of animosity in their dark depths. He had never liked the big, arrogant American but he was not yet ready to challenge his right to be a member of this ragged army.

"This girl, Rico, is the daughter of Señor Richard Wellington. I see you recognize the name. Señor Wellington owns much of the state of California, no? He will no doubt be willing to pay many American dollars to insure the safe return of his pretty daughter."

Ryder looked from Tomás's brutal face to the girl who knelt before him, her hair still clutched in his fist, her body half-exposed to the lustful eyes around her. Her eyes were closed and he could see no trace of emotion on her face but her bound hands were clutched into tight fists against her knees. He could almost feel the nails biting into her palms.

"What do you intend to do with the girl until her father pays the ransom?" He asked the question as if he had only an idle interest in the answer.

Tomás gave her a regretful look and Ryder knew what was in his mind. He wanted the girl, but his mistress of long standing would take a knife to him were he to humiliate her by taking another woman in front of the group. She didn't care what he did outside the camp, but within its confines, she ruled him as firmly as any Latin matron would her husband.

"Perhaps we should draw straws to see who should have her," he suggested, tightening his hold on her hair until Ryder saw one tear slip from the corner of her eye to roll across her cheek.

His hard voice cut across the rising babble of excitement. "I will take the girl." He stepped forward until he faced Tomás across the captive's

14

body. The two men stared at each other for a moment before Ryder spoke again. "The girl is American. I am American. It is right that she should be mine while she is here. Besides," his mouth curved in a crude smile, "as you said, Tomás, it has been a long time since I explored the differences between a man and a woman. I want this one."

For a moment, he thought Tomás would argue. There was a rumble of discontent from the men at his back but he ignored them. If Tomás said the girl was his, none of the others would protest. With a faint shrug, Tomás's eyes dropped and he released his hold on the girl's hair.

"If you want the girl, she is yours, Rico. She is, after all, too skinny to offer a man a soft ride. I prefer a bit of meat with my tortillas."

Ryder nodded once and then turned to look at the other men. His hand fell suggestively near the hilt of the murderous-looking knife in his belt. "Does anyone wish to dispute my claim to the girl?"

There were a few sullen mumbles but no one stepped forward. The norteamericano's skill with a knife was well known. The woman was not worth risking their lives over.

Ryder waited until he was sure there would be no arguments before he bent and hooked his hand roughly around the girl's arm, dragging her to her feet. Her ankles were bound and she would have fallen if he hadn't caught her around the waist. He heard her gasp of pain as he bent and tossed her over his shoulder but he dared show no mercy.

He strode rapidly across the camp to his tent, shouldering open the flap and letting it fall shut behind him. He lowered the girl gently to the cot and then crossed back to the opening and tied the flap securely shut. In a moment he was back at her side, his long fingers going to work on the knot at her wrists.

"Scream your head off."

It was the first words he had addressed to her and she stared at him blankly, her face rigid. He could feel the chill in her flesh and knew that she was in the early stages of shock. But there was no time to baby her. No time to coax her back to life.

He glanced up impatiently. "I'm not going to rape you but I don't want them to know that. You could help by providing a sound track."

She blinked rapidly and then a tinge of hope lightened the gray of her eyes. Ryder winced as the first piercing scream shattered the waiting quiet of the camp, followed a moment later by a second and a third. He growled out a few choice curses in a voice pitched to reach beyond the thin canvas walls and hoped that the noise would be enough to convince those listening.

"I think that should do it. We want them to think I'm raping you, not torturing you." His words were punctuated by her gasp of pain as the ropes fell from her wrists and the blood began to flow into her swollen hands. He quickly unfastened the ropes at her ankles and then took her hands in his and began to rub them gently.

He knew what agony the returning circulation

16

was causing her but other than that initial gasp she was silent. "What's your name?" he asked her, pitching his voice low.

"Cally Stevens."

His head came up sharply. "Stevens? You aren't Wellington's daughter?"

There was a hint of color returning to her cheeks and she pulled her hands away from his to continue the massage herself. "I'm his niece."

"My God," he muttered under his breath, sitting back on his heels and staring at her absently. "The humiliation of making a mistake like this is not going to make Tomás happy. If he finds out he kidnapped the wrong girl . . ." He let his voice trail off. There was no sense in frightening her more than she already was.

"He'll kill me." She finished the sentence with a faint tremor in her voice. Ryder's eyes met hers for a moment and then he nodded slowly.

Cally drew a deep shuddering breath. "Well, then I guess he'll have to continue to think I'm Lisa, won't he?" She flexed her fingers, relieved to find that they still responded to her commands.

She looked at her companion. He had tossed aside his hat and his black hair was tousled, lying across his forehead in a heavy wave. Black brows overshadowed dark blue eyes and a thick mustache concealed his upper lip. Two or three days' growth of beard shadowed strong masculine features. After studying him for a few minutes, she was surprised to find that under the rough exterior was an attractive man.

17

His height alone had been enough to make him stand out from the others. But it was his cool strength, so different from the other men, that had drawn her eyes to him. Then, seeing that he was an accepted member of the group, the fleeting hope that he might help her faded. When he stepped forward and claimed her, she had felt nothing but a vague relief. At least he looked like he took an occasional bath.

"That man out there called you Rico. That doesn't sound very American. Is it a nickname?"

"Of sorts. I'm Ryder Allen. Rico fits in a little better around here."

Cally held out her hand. "It's very nice to meet you."

His mouth quirked upward beneath the thick mustache but he put out his hand to take hers, his much larger palm engulfing her fingers. "I'd return the compliment but you're the last thing I need right now."

She withdrew her hand and tugged futilely at her ruined blouse. "Well, actually, I might have chosen other circumstances myself."

He frowned at the lightness of her tone. Did she realize how much danger she was in?

Cally glanced up in time to catch the disapproval in his eyes. "Would you rather I screamed and cried? I don't think you'd enjoy that much and I can't imagine that it would do any real good." There was a tightness in her voice that told him she was hanging on to her control by the skin of her teeth.

He didn't acknowledge the accuracy of her comment. "How old are you?"

"Twenty-two."

"My God, you're just a kid."

"How old are you?"

"Thirty-eight."

"I've spent most of my life with men considerably older than that. Thirty-eight doesn't seem all that impressive to me. Do you have a safety pin or something that I could use to hold this together?"

He looked at her efforts critically, shrugging off his feelings of unreality. This was not the kind of conversation that he would have envisioned having with a terrified young girl. But she was right, hysterics would get them nowhere. In fact, if she had been the hysterical type, he would probably have smacked her.

"The blouse is ruined. There's no sense in trying to repair it. Besides, it hardly fits with my image of a brutal rapist to be providing you with safety pins, which I don't have anyway. You can wear one of my shirts."

She eyed the width of his shoulders but didn't comment. If the shirt hung on her, so much the better. She had no desire to draw attention to herself. She took the shirt he handed her. Her gray eyes met his levelly. "What do you plan to do with me?"

Ryder shook his head, running his fingers through his already tousled hair. "I don't know exactly. You'll be safe enough for a while. There's nobody here who's going to risk my temper. Tomás would be the only possibility and his woman would kill him before she'd let him take another mistress."

"Well, that's a relief but it's still only a temporary solution."

She kept any doubts she might have about him to herself but he didn't have to be a mind reader to know that she had plenty of them. He didn't blame her. She'd be a fool not to have reservations about him.

"Yes, I know." He felt an irrational annoyance at the victim in this mess. She was a threat to everything he had been working toward.

"Will your uncle or your parents pay the ransom?"

Her fingers tightened on his shirt and her eyes dropped from his face as she slowly shook her head. "My parents are dead. I don't know if Uncle Richard will pay. He's always said that he would never pay a kidnapper because it never does any good but this is the first time it's actually happened. It doesn't really matter though, because Tomás doesn't plan on returning me alive, with or without the ransom. I heard the men talking about it in the truck."

Ryder glanced down, seeing her fingers knotted in the fabric of his shirt. So she was not totally without nerves.

"You speak Spanish? Does Tomás know that?"

She shook her head. "I don't think so. Any time he spoke to me, he used English."

"Let's keep it that way. At least for now."

She looked down at the shirt and then back up at him, uncertainty and a hint of pleading in her eyes. With a twisted smile, he got up and ostentatiously turned his back to her, taking a step away to pick up his canteen. He could easily have reached it from where he was sitting but he didn't begrudge her need for at least the illusion of privacy.

Cally quickly shrugged out of the ruined silk blouse and slid her arms into the dark cotton shirt. She kept her eyes trained on her host's broad back, taking inventory of the heavy muscles that corded his shoulders.

What was he going to do with her? He had saved her from the certainty of brutal rape, massaged her hands with a gentleness that was at odds with both his appearance and the company he seemed to keep, and now he had turned his back to give her a moment's privacy. An odd man to find in this situation.

The shirt was much too large, of course but, after a brief struggle, she wiggled her hands free of the sleeves and pulled the front together. But her fingers were still numb and stiff and they refused to grip a button, let alone force it through the tiny slot meant for it. This minor frustration was the last straw and she blinked hard against the sting of tears. She was not going to cry over a damned button! She sniffed as a tear slid down her cheek, quickly followed by another.

Ryder turned around as she made a frustrated little noise. She clutched the shirt together over her fragile breasts and gave him a helpless look, mingled with slightly tremulous amusement, and a tinge of defiance, as if daring him to notice her tears.

"It was very gentlemanly of you to turn your back. Unfortunately, my fingers don't seem to be working right."

He was more touched by those two lonely tears than he would have been by dramatic sobs. The girl had guts.

He sat down in front of her and quickly buttoned the shirt, his callused fingers impersonal. More brisk movements rolled the sleeves, leaving her hands free. He acknowledged her murmured thank-you with a nod and handed her the canteen.

She took it eagerly. Her mouth felt dry and cracked. The water was warm and tasted faintly of the chemicals used to purify it, but never had a liquid tasted so wonderful. She took two swallows, letting it trickle down her parched throat. She longed to gulp down more. The way she felt right now, she could empty the canteen and still feel thirsty. But she forced herself to lower the canteen, her eyes meeting his with a faint question.

His brows rose in surprise and he gestured for her to drink again. "Go ahead. Water is not a big problem. Just be sure and don't drink anything that hasn't been treated." She thought she read a hint of approval in those compelling eyes but she wasn't sure.

He waited until she handed the canteen back to him before speaking again. "How did Tomás manage to get hold of you instead of your cousin? He may not be the most brilliant of men but he doesn't make mistakes of this magnitude. He wouldn't have stayed alive as long as he has if he did."

Cally shifted slightly, trying to find a softer spot but the ground beneath the tent was uncompromisingly hard. Her hands still itched with renewed circulation and her head spun with exhaustion and fear but she was alive and, for now, reasonably safe.

"Uncle Richard had business in the capital. He's financing a new processing plant on the coast."

Ryder nodded. "I had heard that there was an American company building a factory but I didn't get a name."

"Uncle Richard prefers to keep his name out of the news. This plant is going to provide a lot of jobs but not much money for the company, at least not for a while. The newspapers like to see him as some kind of modern-day Robin Hood and it makes Uncle Richard uncomfortable. Not that he isn't a bit of a philanthropist but there are tax benefits in building a plant like this. Anyway, he really hates the publicity so he tries to keep his name out of the news as much as possible."

"So Richard Wellington is a practical prince among industrialists. That doesn't explain why he brought you with him. Doesn't he realize how volatile the situation is down here?"

"You may find this hard to believe, but the reports the rest of the world has been getting have implied that everything is just fine here. The government is in control, land reform is going through without too many problems, and everybody is happy. There's been no mention of your friend Tomás and his little band of guerrillas."

"Tomás has more than a 'little band of guerrillas.' He's got a small army. But he has laid pretty low. There've been no pitched battles, no major attacks. Yes, I can see the government keeping this quiet." He ran his fingers through his hair and Cally could almost smell the restless tension in his big frame. If there had been room, he would have been pacing back and forth.

"I didn't say that the reports were swallowed hook, line, and sinker. Most people who follow the news have doubts about everything being quite as perfect as the government would like us to think."

"And that brings us back to the original question. Why did your uncle bring you into a potentially dangerous situation like this?"

"It was my fault," she admitted. "I fast-talked my way into coming along with him."

"I wouldn't think that a tiny Central American country that's perpetually on the brink of revolution would have much to interest a young girl."

Cally shrugged. "My dad was an archaeologist. He did some work in this area a long time ago. He always described the place with great fondness. I've got the summer off and Uncle Richard was coming here. It seemed like a perfect opportunity. Believe me, if I'd had any idea just what the situation was like, I would have stayed at home."

"How did Tomás get hold of you?"

"I wanted to go to the outskirts of the capital. There are some ruins that Dad worked on only a few hours' drive away. Uncle Richard didn't want me to go but I can be pretty bullheaded. This is one time when I should have listened to him. I hired a couple of guides and I guess I should have checked their references more thoroughly. But I'm not sure who I could have asked. It's a little hard to get auto club recommendations down here.

"We were only an hour or so out of the capital when Tomás and his merry men stopped the jeep and my trustworthy guides calmly handed me over to them in exchange for a rather large wad of money. Maybe I should be flattered that I'm worth so much. Of course, they thought I was Lisa so I can't really take it personally."

"Tomás plans on getting a huge ransom from Wellington. Whatever he paid to get hold of you is a pittance compared to what he expects to get from your uncle. How did the mix-up occur between you and your cousin?"

"Probably just because I'm traveling with Uncle Richard. Lisa travels with him fairly often. We're both blond and about the same age. My 'guides' called me Señorita Wellington a couple of times. I corrected them once but I don't think they grasped that I wasn't who they thought I was. At the time, it didn't seem to matter that much."

"Well, it's going to matter a whole lot if Tomás finds out that he's got the wrong girl," Ryder warned her. "As long as you're in camp, you'll answer to the name Lisa or Wellington. Tomás's

25

pride is at stake and, if he finds out who you are, he may decide that the best way to salvage it is to turn you over to the men before he has you killed."

He felt an unfamiliar twinge of regret when the color drained away from her face, leaving her ashen. He had the urge to reassure her but he resisted it. Better that she face facts. Neither of them could afford a careless mistake. Besides, he wasn't going to make any false promises. Maybe he couldn't protect her. He had a job to do and that had to come first.

Even as the thought occurred to him he knew, with a mixture of irritation and resignation, that he would protect her or die trying. Important as his job here was, he couldn't stand back and let them kill her. He fumbled for a pack of cigarettes.

"Who are you, Ryder Allen? Why are you helping me?"

"I'm an American. Maybe I just had a surge of patriotic feeling."

She was already shaking her head. "No, there's more to it than that. You talk as if you're an observer, not a participant in this organization."

His eyes flickered briefly and his fingers tightened around the cigarette. She was a little too clever to be safe. "If you're half as smart as you think you are, you'll keep your mouth shut and your ideas to yourself. I've helped you at considerable risk to myself and my position here. I could just as easily change my mind."

His tone was flat, all the more frightening for its

lack of force and Cally shivered, feeling chilled despite the stifling heat in the tent.

His eyes narrowed on her through a thin veil of smoke. "You'll obey me in all things. If I tell you to jump, your only question is 'how high.' Understand?"

He waited to see her nod of understanding. "Good. I'm going to leave you alone for a while. Get some rest. Stay quiet and don't leave the tent. I'll bring you some food when I get a chance."

He tossed her a tube of antiseptic cream before standing up. "Put some of that on your wrists and anywhere else you've got an open wound. Infection is the last thing you need."

He stopped to pick up his hat and crush it onto his head. Cally watched his movements from beneath lowered lids. Inside, she was a turmoil of conflicting emotions. He frightened her but he offered the only hope of safety in an uncertain world. She was terrified as she watched him walk to the flap. What if he didn't come back?

He hesitated for a moment, his back to her and then turned slowly. His dark eyes skimmed her tense features. "Don't worry too much. I'll take care of you." The words were gruff, as if torn from some core of softness that was unfamiliar to him.

Cally smiled, willing her lips to be steady and raised her hand in a mocking salute. "Yes, sir."

His mustache twitched in a reluctant smile and then he was gone, leaving her alone with her fears.

CHAPTER TWO

The hours passed slowly but Cally wasn't complaining. In her current situation, she'd rather be bored and safe than entertained. Besides, boredom wasn't exactly the word to use. It was difficult to be bored when she knew that every hour could be her last.

For a long time after Ryder left, she sat on the cot staring at the opposite wall of the tent, teeth clenched against the convulsive shudders that racked her small frame. She had come so close to dying. The danger wasn't over yet but this was a tiny island of safety.

She rubbed her hands together absently. Just how long this would remain safe was a question she couldn't even begin to answer. Ryder Allen. He was the only thing standing between her and Tomás. She had no way of knowing how solid a barrier he would make. If he was really one of this ragged army, then she could not depend on him at all. He could have protected her on a whim and he could throw her to the wolves if his mood changed.

If he was an agent for the government, she couldn't count on him to put her safety ahead of his job. His protection would extend only as far as it could without jeopardizing his assignment here.

No, she was grateful for what he had done so far and she would cooperate with him up to a point, but when push came to shove, she knew she couldn't depend on anybody but herself. After all, she was the one who had something to lose. Her life couldn't possibly mean much to Ryder, no matter who he was.

She glanced at her wrist and then remembered that one of the kidnappers had taken her watch sometime during the interminable ride here. But it was still only late afternoon. Uncle Richard wouldn't even have missed her yet. In fact, if she didn't return tonight, there was no guarantee that he would be worried. He might just think that she had decided to spend the night at the ruins, despite his warnings about the dangers of doing that. Her lips twisted ruefully. There were definite disadvantages to having a reputation for ignoring advice.

Now, if she had been a little more like her cousin Lisa, she wouldn't have dismissed Uncle Richard's advice about sticking close to the capital and she would be safe and sound in their hotel. In fact, if she had taken Uncle Richard's advice, she wouldn't have come on this trip at all.

Poor Uncle Richard. Her smile deepened. He had such a hard time coping with her. He could never understand why she had to do things her own way. To tell the truth, she wasn't sure why either. She just couldn't stand to sit by and let someone else direct her life.

She glanced around the tent. If you could read a person from their surroundings, what did this place tell her about Ryder Allen? That he was very tidy but not much else. Everything was neatly in place but there was nothing of a personal nature. No pictures, no books, nothing that said anything about him. There was a duffel bag in one corner and she eyed it speculatively. No. For the moment he was the closest thing to an ally she had. She wouldn't risk antagonizing him by searching his things. The way her luck had been going today, he would catch her at it and shoot her on the spot.

But she'd go crazy if she didn't have something to do, something to focus on besides the situation she was in. There was deck of cards sitting on the wooden crate that functioned as a table and she leaned over and picked them up. Surely he wouldn't object to her using his cards.

When Ryder entered the tent just before dark, he found his—guest? prisoner?—sitting cross-legged on the cot, dealing out a hand of solitaire. It was easy to see that she wasn't really thinking about what she was doing. Her attention was focused inward, as if she were trying to find strength inside. She looked so young, so fragile that he had a moment of disbelief. It wasn't possible that she was there. This was a bizarre dream brought on by too many months in the sun. Too many months of pressure.

He tugged off his hat and tossed it onto the foot

of the cot. Her head jerked up, her gray eyes wide. He saw the fear replaced by a cautious smile as she recognized him and he had to restrain the urge to curse long and loud. He didn't want her to smile at him and give him her trust. It reminded him of things he had forgotten. Things he had given up years ago and could never have again. Home. Family. Warmth. Love. He shook his head irritably, running his fingers through his hair. He *had* been out in the sun too long.

Cally's hands came up automatically, catching the fruit he tossed in her direction. Her stomach rumbled as the sweet smell of ripe banana reached her. She hadn't realized how hungry she was until food was within reach. She closed her eyes in ecstasy as she chewed the first bite.

She swallowed and opened her eyes, giving him a wide smile. For an instant, she glimpsed something in his eyes that was half pleasure, half pain. A hunger fully as great as her own, but not physical. Something stirred inside and she had the urge to reach out. But the expression was gone so quickly that she might have imagined it. His eyes revealed nothing. Dark blue mirrors that reflected her back upon herself.

"Thanks. My stomach thought my throat had been cut."

"I'm sorry it isn't more." He lowered himself into a camp chair and Cally held her breath, waiting to see the flimsy canvas and wood frame collapse beneath his weight. She caught a fleeting glimpse of amusement in his face. "It's stronger than it looks."

She grinned. "I guess it would have to be." She returned her attention to her banana, biting into the fruit with the healthy appetite of a young animal.

"Being kidnapped doesn't seem to have ruined your appetite," he commented mildly. Her apparent unconcern was irritating. Didn't she know how precarious her position was?

"My father dragged my mother and me all over the world. When I was ten Mother died, and then I traveled alone with him. He was a good man but he wasn't very practical and we visited some pretty out-of-the-way places. I learned to eat and sleep whenever I got the chance because I never knew where the next meal was going to come from." She shrugged. "I'd probably enjoy this meal a lot more if I were safely in my hotel room but, since I can't have that, I'm going to enjoy every bite of what I have."

His dark brows came together slightly. He couldn't argue with her logic but there was something unnatural about her calm. He pushed the thought aside. He should be thanking God that she wasn't the hysterical type.

"Your next meal will be in about two hours. Tomás has demanded your presence at the evening meal."

She froze for a moment, a frisson running up her spine. "I suppose that's the local equivalent of an invitation to the White House? I couldn't just say 'no thank you'?"

"It's not an invitation, it's an order. The only acceptable reason for you not to go would be if I'd abused you so badly that you couldn't move." He watched the color flood up into her pale skin and felt a twinge of regret for embarrassing her. "It's not worth risking the lie just to avoid Tomás."

She nodded, swallowing the last of the banana before tossing the peel neatly into the garbage can. Her face lit in a pleased smile at this small success. At least everything in her life wasn't going against her, though the minor triumph of hitting the can wasn't going to do her much good unless there was a talent scout for the LA Lakers lurking in the underbrush.

Ryder felt again that twinge of unwanted emotion as he saw her reaction. He reached for his cigarettes and lit one with impatience. He was aware of Cally's gray eyes flickering over his face and he wondered what she saw there. Whatever it was, she picked up the cards without comment and dealt out another hand of solitaire.

He drew deeply, feeling the smoke fill his lungs before he exhaled slowly. He watched her hands move over the cards, shifting a red jack onto a black queen and then the five of clubs onto the six of diamonds. What was she thinking? *Still waters run deep.* The old phrase popped into his head and he suspected the description fit her quite well. There was more going on beneath that calm surface than met the eye.

Twenty-two. Hardly old enough to be let out alone at night. Of course, when he was that age, he had been carrying a tommy gun through the jungles of Vietnam. Cally Stevens looked as pale and fragile as the Peace roses his mother had always grown in her rose garden.

He shook aside the memories of warm summer evenings when the air was filled with the heady scent of roses and took another drag on the cigarette, letting the acrid smoke banish the last traces of imaginary scent. Her hands were delicate, the nails short and unpainted, the fingers slender and graceful as they manipulated the worn cards.

"You missed the red seven on the black eight." His husky voice was unexpected. Despite the fact that Cally was painfully aware of his presence, hearing him speak startled her. She moved the card he had indicated, flipping over the eight of clubs, which was the card she needed to break the impasse she had reached. In a matter of minutes, the game was over, all the cards neatly stacked according to suit.

She picked them up and began to shuffle, allowing her eyes to drift to his hard features. "Thanks. I hadn't seen that and I was about to give up."

"You'd have seen it sooner or later."

"Maybe. Maybe you're just good luck for me." Though the words were light, Ryder reacted as if stung. He leaned over to crush out the cigarette butt in the shallow can that served as an ashtray, his movements quick and irritated.

"Don't bet on it." He got to his feet. "I'll be back to take you to dinner." Cally's eyes were wide as she looked up at him, then nervously brushed her tangled hair back from her face. His eyes darkened with annoyance and some other emotion she couldn't define and he leaned across the cot to snatch up his duffel bag, rummaging in its depths briefly before coming up with a comb, which he tossed into her lap.

Without another word, he turned and left the tent, leaving her staring wide-eyed and uncertain after him.

She was still uncertain of his mood when he returned to the tent almost two hours later. In the time he was gone, she had plenty of time to remind herself that she couldn't depend on him, couldn't count on him for anything, except possibly that he wouldn't do her any harm himself. He might be willing to look the other way if she found an opportunity to escape, but that was a very big maybe.

If Ryder sensed her uncertain state of mind, he didn't say anything, either to add to it or to reassure her. His eyes were coolly impersonal as they skimmed over her. His shirt covered her from neck to knees, providing a loose, voluminous camouflage for the slender curves of her body. She had spent almost an hour working his comb through her hair and now it fell in shining waves down her back, a beacon of silvery gold in the dusty light of the tent.

"You'll do." He reached out to catch her chin

35

between thumb and forefinger and tilted her face into the light. "I'm notoriously kind to women and children," he murmured sardonically. "But even *I* couldn't have accomplished a rape without leaving a bruise or two and your face is unmarked."

Cally's heart almost stopped as he lifted his free hand. She caught her breath on a stifled half sob and shut her eyes, squeezing them tight as she braced herself.

Ryder rubbed his fingers over the inside of the old chimney lamp that hung on a hook from the ceiling and then turned back to the girl. He froze, his eyes narrowing as he took in her paralyzed condition. She looked as frightened as a doe caught in the beam of a hunter's light.

It took only a moment to realize that she thought he was going to strike her. The realization brought a confusing tangle of emotions. Anger ran through him with surprising force. She had no reason to think that he was going to hit her, but she had no reason to think he *wouldn't* hit her. On the heels of this thought came admiration. She expected a blow and she was frightened but she hadn't cried out or tried to evade it.

Cally released her breath in a rush, her eyes flying open as his fingers brushed gently along her cheekbone. His expression was intent as he took his fingers from her cheek to her jaw, once again rubbing the skin with delicate strokes that went oddly with his rough exterior.

He finished whatever he was doing and his eyes met hers. Reading her confusion, he lifted his hand to display the smoky residue that coated his fingers before he wiped his hand on the leg of his worn jeans. He released her chin and Cally felt herself go weak with relief.

"Bruises," she whispered shakily.

"Bruises." His eyes continued to dwell on her face. "You thought I was going to hit you, didn't you?"

She gave a laugh that stopped just short of tears. "Well, you did say I had to look authentic. I thought maybe you were a method actor and figured the only good bruise was a real bruise. How was I to know you were into greasepaint?"

She lifted her hand to her cheek but he caught her fingers before she could touch the skin. Electricity shot from her hand into her arm, weaving a tingling path across her shoulders and down her spine. Her eyes widened and she read some of the same surprise in his before thick black lashes covered his expression. His hand released hers.

"Leave it," he ordered gruffly. "Smudgy fingerprints aren't going to add to the realistic look."

She nodded, absently rubbing her still tingling fingers together. "I'm not quite sure what's expected of me. I mean is this a formal meal where I've got to remember which fork is which?"

"Tomás just wants to gloat over you a bit. He likes the idea of having a wealthy American woman in his power. It makes him feel like a big man. Considering all you're supposed to have been through today, you don't have to do anything but look subdued. Remember that your name is Lisa

37

Wellington and you don't speak the language. No matter what is said, don't respond. Do exactly what I tell you and if you can summon up a few terrified looks in my direction, it wouldn't hurt. Keep in mind, I'm supposed to have brutally raped you just a few hours ago."

She nodded, feeling her stomach muscles tighten as he gave her one last critical look and then opened the tent flap. His fingers closed around her upper arm as he led her out into the dim light of early evening.

When she was brought here, the camp had been concealed from her, first by the high walls of the truck, then by the more frightening wall of men. Now, she kept her head down but stole looks at her surroundings. The more knowledge she had, the better chance of escaping.

What she saw was not encouraging. Tomás might be a short, ugly little braggart but he did not believe in leaving his camp unprotected. Tents and crude huts huddled together in a rough circle. Outside the circle of buildings a wall of brush stood between the camp and the jungle. Primitive but effective. Not only would the thick brush be difficult to penetrate, it would be impossible to force a way through it without making enough noise to wake the dead. Several guards carrying wicked-looking rifles patrolled the perimeter inside the brush.

Before she had time to consider the information her covert studies had given her, Ryder was leading her up a short set of rickety stairs and into a small house that looked as if it had been built before the Flood. The screen door opened with a whine of hinges that set her teeth on edge and then she was blinking in what seemed like an overpowering amount of light.

Once her eyes adjusted, she saw that the light was provided by a pair of Coleman lanterns that hung from the ceiling, spilling clarity over a room that would have been better left in the dark.

"Señorita Wellington, how wonderful to have you in my home." Tomás swaggered across the filthy wooden floor, his thumbs hooked in his belt, his greasy features wreathed in a gloating smile.

Cally kept her head down, feeling her stomach twist in a knot that was a mixture of hatred and fear. Ryder kept his fingers wrapped around her arm and she drew what comfort she could from that contact, though for all she knew, he offered as great a threat as the swaggering little bully in front of them.

"You do not look happy, señorita. Perhaps Rico has not been treating you well?" His fingers came out to catch her chin, tilting her face into the light. Cally held her breath, her lashes concealing the revulsion in her eyes. Tomás studied her face, the pallor that owed nothing to artifice, and the faint gray bruising that marked her cheek and jaw. Would he see through to the unmarked skin beneath the primitive makeup? Her knees almost buckled with relief when he released her to turn a mock reproachful look on Ryder.

"Rico, our guest is pale. Perhaps you have been

too hard on her. A man who has been a long time without a woman sometimes forgets how to treat them."

Ryder glanced at his silent captive indifferently. "I haven't forgotten, Tomás."

Cally flinched back as Tomás reached out to stroke one filthy thumb across her cheek. "Such soft skin. Like the petals of a flower."

She risked a glance upward and cringed inwardly at the avid lust in Tomás's eyes. It was all she could do to keep from slapping his hand away. Ryder's fingers tightened on her arm as if in warning and she stood silent.

Ryder could feel the quiver of revulsion that shook Cally's slim body. That didn't surprise him. Most women would find Tomás less than appetizing. Seeing the other man's hand on her brought a hard knot of anger to his gut. His eyes narrowed.

"Where is Elena, Tomás? I'm surprised she isn't here to greet your guests."

The mention of his mistress acted like salt on a wound with Tomás. His hand left Cally's face as if scalded and he cast a furtive glance over his shoulder. Seeing that they were still alone, he gave Ryder an acid look but he stepped back, leaving Cally to breathe easier.

"Elena is still getting dressed. You know how it is with women." He shrugged broadly. As he spoke, the sharp tap of heels approached the room.

Elena did not just walk into the room. She made an entrance worthy of Gloria Swanson. She paused in the doorway with all the poise and grace of a woman who is sure that she is the center of attention, which indeed she was. Tomás looked at her with an expression of stunned admiration. Cally was simply stunned.

A glorious mane of shining black hair framed a face that was sulkily beautiful. Everything about Elena pouted. Her lips, painted a brilliant scarlet, were set in a permanent pout. Her lids drooped over dark eyes, almost weighed down by the longest false eyelashes Cally had ever seen. Her sloping shoulders were bared by the neckline of a purple and red satin dress that would have been the envy of any circus tent owner. The ruffled neck stopped just short of baring her nipples, leaving one with the definite feeling that at any moment it might slip and bare all. Ridiculously high red heels and black fish-net hose completed the outfit, along with long scarlet nails.

It should have looked ridiculous. It *did* look ridiculous but it was also magnificently flamboyant and exotic and her attitude of sulky indifference left Cally with the feeling that she had never seen anyone quite so spectacular. It was only after some of the dazzle had worn off that she noticed the dirt on the woman's arms, the spots of grease on the brilliantly colored dress and Elena's constant scratching which gave Cally an uneasy feeling that she should have brought a flea collar.

Tomás however saw none of these minor flaws. It took him a moment to recover his breath and then he rushed across the room to seize her hand, planting a passionate kiss on the palm that was

41

received with the same indifference Elena apparently bestowed on the rest of the world.

"My darling, you look magnificent as always." He stared at her as if blinded by her magnificence and her eyes flickered over his face before going beyond his shoulder to where Ryder and Cally stood.

"You are embarrassing me, Tomás. We have guests."

Cally kept her lashes down, observing the rest of the room through their fragile shield. She thought, but could not be certain, that the look Elena gave Ryder held more than a hint of invitation. If so, Ryder gave no sign that he had received the message. His fingers tugged on Cally's arm as he led her forward to meet her hostess.

"Rico, it has been a long time since we have seen you. You have been keeping too much to yourself. Soon you will forget how to be civilized." Elena fluttered those incredible lashes and Cally was lost in admiration, amazed that the woman could even lift her eyelids beneath their weight, let alone flutter them.

Tomás looked less than happy about her coquettish smile for the other man. "That's what I told him, Elena. And I think he agreed because he spent a large part of the afternoon hidden away in his tent with our guest. Perhaps she was teaching you manners, ay, Rico?" He laughed heartily at his joke, apparently undisturbed by the fact that no one else was visibly amused.

Elena had tried to pretend that Cally didn't exist

42

but Tomás's words made that impossible and she turned her eyes to the other woman. In a matter of seconds, Cally was assessed, weighed, filed under "no contest," and dismissed. In other circumstances, it would have been difficult to hold back open laughter. Even under these conditions, there was an irrepressible imp inside that was amused.

The evening could only improve from there, Cally thought and, to a certain extent, she was right. Once Elena entered the room, Cally was saved from any more of Tomás's attentions. Elena made it clear that Tomás was her personal property and neither he nor anyone else should have any ideas to the contrary. Cally had the feeling that she would like to have applied the same rules to Ryder.

The chicken stew, served by one of the other women who lived in the camp, was simple but tasty and Cally ate hungrily. She didn't utter a word during the entire meal, which earned Ryder several compliments from Tomás, who seemed to feel that this was a sign that Ryder had put the fear of God in her.

Elena also had little to say. Her pose of decadent, slightly tarnished elegance slipped further when the food appeared. She might be indifferent to Tomás's affections but the lure of spicy stew was a different story. Cally watched from out of the corner of her eye, awed by the amount of food the other woman managed to put away, as well as her complete disregard for anything resembling table manners.

At the end of the meal, Tomás leaned back and lit a huge cigar that resembled a pagan phallic symbol. Ryder lit a cigarette. Elena picked irritably at the food left on her plate and Cally had the feeling that she was considering scavenging in the kitchen, as if she hadn't just eaten enough to feed a small army. Cally kept her hands in her lap and her eyes down, wondering when the royal audience was going to end, wanting nothing so much as a hot bath, a soft bed and to wake up and find this had all been a bad dream.

"Have you sent a ransom demand to Wellington?" Ryder's question brought Cally out of the dazed stupor that had been creeping over her. Just in time, she remembered that she was not supposed to understand the language and she kept her head from jerking up. Tension gripped her as she waited for Tomás's answer.

"Tomorrow. By then he will have had time to worry about his pretty daughter. When we tell him that she is safe, he will be so grateful that he will not argue with our requests."

"It wouldn't hurt to give him even more time to worry."

"One would think you were in no hurry to get rid of the girl, Rico. Perhaps you have discovered that she has her uses, yes?"

Ryder's eyes skimmed coolly across Cally's bent head. Tension fairly shimmered around her. It was time to bring this charade to an end. She had done well so far, but there was a limit to what he could expect. He ground his cigarette out in his plate and got to his feet, reaching down to pull Cally to hers, again his fingers wrapped around her arm in a harsh grip.

"As you say, she has her uses. Elena, thank you for the meal."

Elena roused herself from the bones she was picking and gave him a sultry smile, only slightly spoiled by the bits of pepper caught between her front teeth. "You should visit more often, Rico. *Mi casa es su casa.*"

And it wasn't just her *casa* she was offering, Cally thought cynically, wondering why the thought irritated her.

It seemed typical of the man that Elena's invitation went right over Tomás's head. He was too much of an egotist to suspect anything. He blew out a huge cloud of nauseating smoke and laughed heartily. "Rico is unlikely to be visiting our home, Elena, my sweet. Not while he has other things to occupy him. Just remember, Rico, do not use her too roughly. We may need to show her in good shape before we get the ransom from her father. Make sure any damage is where it will not show." He was still chuckling when Ryder led Cally out of the dirty little house and into the compound.

Cally held on to her anger until they were back in Ryder's tent, the flap securely tied behind them.

"That man is the most disgusting little worm it has ever been my misfortune to meet. I don't know how you can stand to be around him, no matter who you're working for. Not even the C . . ."

"Shut up!"

45

His hands snapped out to catch her shoulders and administer a hard shake, breaking her words off in mid-breath. Cally stopped, her eyes wide as he drew her up on her toes and leaned down to look directly into her face. The dim light of the kerosene lamp cast long shadows across his features, giving him a Mephistophelian look that made her remember how little she knew of him. In contrast to Tomás, he had, for a little while, seemed to represent safety, but that wasn't necessarily true.

"You don't seem to grasp your position here. You're only alive and unharmed because Tomás needs you and I had a brief spurt of compassion. I've told you I'll help you but only if you keep your mouth shut and obey me implicitly. If you get careless; if you say a word out of place; if you so much as blink crosswise, you could get us both killed. Understand?"

Cally nodded, not trusting her voice to remain steady. Ryder continued to stare into her eyes, as if trying to see into her thoughts. After a moment, he gave a rough exclamation and released her, turning away to pick up his sleeping bag.

"You sleep on the cot. I'll use the sleeping bag."

Cally crept over to the cot and sat on its edge, watching as he unrolled the sleeping bag on the canvas-covered ground near the door.

"You'll be more comfortable without your clothes." He threw her one last glance before turning the lamp wick down, plunging the tent into darkness. Cally could hear him moving around,

46

the thud as his jeans hit the ground. He was obviously taking his own advice. She hesitated a long moment before unbuttoning her pants and slipping them off. Modesty had its place, but right now it wasn't going to gain her a comfortable night's sleep. She kept his shirt on, however, unwilling to part with its soft comfort.

The cot was not too uncomfortable, she realized as she lay down on it. There was a small pillow at its head and a thin blanket lay across the foot. If she could ignore the lumps in the pillow, the holes in the blanket and the unyielding surface of the cot itself, she could almost imagine that she was in her own bed. Her lips twisted in a rueful smile that broke apart on a quiver of fear.

She turned on her side, drawing her knees up to her chest and curling around herself in a primal response to the situation. She took deep breaths, trying to fight down the suffocating waves of terror that threatened to overwhelm her. This afternoon, alone in this same tent, she had been able to control her fear by giving thanks for the fact that she was still alive and relatively unharmed. But now, in the darkness, with the mysterious Ryder Allen a few feet away, she couldn't console herself with that anymore.

In some ways, his presence only made things worse. Could she trust him? Depend on him? Or was she totally on her own? Was he one of Tomás's men? Was he an agent sent to infiltrate this shabby army? And if he was, was that fact going to do her any good?

The questions spun round and round in her thoughts until she felt dizzy. She was frightened. She blinked rapidly to force back tears. Crying wasn't going to do any good. But the tears continued to fall and all her mental exhortations failed to stem the flood. With a soft sob, she turned her face into the hard lumpy pillow and began to cry out some of the terror of the day.

Across the tent, Ryder lay with eyes wide open, staring at the night-black canvas above him. When the quiet sobbing finally stopped and her ragged breathing told him that she slept, he reached for his cigarettes and lit one, cursing softly at the faint tremor in his fingers. He shook out the match angrily, and dropped it in the ashtray.

Damn it all to hell! Just a few more weeks and he would have been finished here. He would have had all the information he needed. Tomás was planning a move against the government, something bigger than anything that had gone before. An alliance with another guerrilla band and surreptitious aid from Cuba would provide him with enough strength to bring the long-standing unofficial war into the open. Once Ryder had the details, he could disappear on a visit to the capital and arrange for word of his death in a barroom brawl to filter back to Tomás.

Now he had to decide what to do with Ms. Cally Stevens. If he could somehow buy an extra week or two, he might be able to get the information out of Tomás. If it came down to the wire, he could risk breaking into the shack where Tomás held his war councils. Somewhere in that shack, he kept records and plans. The place was always guarded, but if he had to, he could get in.

Cally drew a shuddering breath and murmured in her sleep and Ryder's fingers tightened around the cigarette. He would start smuggling food and supplies out of the camp tomorrow. There was no telling when they might have to leave in a hurry. Everything hinged on how Richard Wellington responded to the ransom note. If the man had the sense to stall for a while, Ryder might have time to get the plans *and* get himself and Cally out alive.

He stubbed out the cigarette and shut his eyes. Whatever was going to happen, he might as well get a decent night's sleep while he could.

But his sleep was restless, broken by dreams of silken hair that cascaded through his fingers like cool water and the scent of roses on a warm summer night.

CHAPTER THREE

When Cally awoke the next morning, she was alone. She sat up on the cot and brushed the hair back from her face, grimacing at the ache in her back. The cot would definitely not qualify for the Hilton good-bed award. Still, all things considered, she'd had an amazingly good night's sleep. All the years of traveling with her father helped. She'd learned early in life to sleep anywhere, under any conditions.

Ryder's sleeping bag was neatly rolled and sitting at the foot of the cot. On the crate that served as a table, there was a chipped pottery plate holding a stack of tortillas and lying next to those was a papaya and a small bunch of bananas. She reached out and picked up a tortilla. It was still warm from the grill and she gave silent thanks to her absent host as she rolled it and bit into it.

With daylight, her spirits rose slightly. Things didn't look quite as black in the morning as they had the night before. By the time she had eaten three tortillas and the papaya, she was beginning to wonder where Ryder was. It didn't matter how many times she told herself that she couldn't depend on him, he represented the closest thing to an ally that she had and she felt better when he was near.

She slipped on her jeans, brushing futilely at the dirt that marked the knees. With a shrug, she abandoned them as hopeless and picked up the comb Ryder had tossed her the day before. She worked the sturdy plastic teeth through her hair, then braided the extravagant length and worked a strong thread loose from the edge of the blanket to tie the end of the braid before tossing it over her shoulder.

She lay back on the cot, resting her head on her folded hands and stared up at the canvas. What was she going to do? Uncle Richard had always said that he wouldn't pay a ransom. If he stuck by that . . . But did it really matter? Whether he paid it or not, her captors didn't intend to let her live. She'd seen too much. Would Ryder stand by and let them execute her? She shook the question off, irritated by the way her mind insisted on casting him in the role of good guy. Why?

Before she could begin to come up with an answer, the flap was pushed inward and Ryder stepped through. Cally sat up, her eyes wary. His mood the night before had been uncertain, to say the least. She wasn't sure what to expect from him now. He set a newly filled canteen on the floor near the cot before looking at her. His expression was hard to read but Cally decided to assume the best.

"Thanks for the breakfast." One slim hand gestured gracefully toward the crate.

"No problem. The food is monotonous but there's plenty of it."

"Any new word from my gracious host?"

"He's planning on sending a ransom note to your 'father' this afternoon. He expects to have a reply sometime tomorrow. He's giving Wellington a week to come up with the gold."

She swallowed, lowering her eyes so that he couldn't read their expression. "A week. Not very long. Does he plan on getting rid of me as soon as he's got the money?"

Ryder shrugged. "I don't know." He dropped down to sit cross-legged on the floor, pulling cigarettes out of one pocket of his safari shirt as he did so. He lit one and took a deep drag before speaking again. "Tomás is being pretty closemouthed about this whole thing. A lot depends on what Wellington does when he gets the note. If he can come up with a way to stall . . ." A shrug finished the sentence.

Cally wrapped her hands around her upper arms, hugging herself to ward off a sudden chill that had nothing to do with the temperature.

Watching her, Ryder felt that annoying surge of emotion again. He inhaled deeply on the cigarette, trying to burn the feeling away with the harsh smoke. But it persisted, urging him to reassure her, to tell her that he'd protect her. But he couldn't do that. He couldn't promise her anything. He might not be able to accomplish anything but getting himself killed along with her.

His eyes sharpened as she scratched absently at an insect bite on her arm. "Don't scratch."

Cally jumped at his barked words, her gaze refocusing on him. She had been so wrapped up in tangled thoughts and unformed plans that she had almost forgotten his presence. He leaned forward and took her hand, turning her arm until he could see the small red welt on her forearm. She stared at his bent head, confused by the tingle of awareness that ran up her arm, creating a fluttering in her chest.

"Mosquito," he muttered under his breath. "I should have thought." He released her arm and sat back. "I've been in the tropics so long, I hardly notice them anymore, especially in the dry season. Tonight, I'll get you some netting and you can wrap it around yourself. Mosquito bites down here are nothing to mess around with."

"I had all my shots," she offered.

"Unfortunately, not all of the mosquitoes in this area have heard that the shots are supposed to protect you. There are still some strains of malaria that are resistant to the vaccines. It's best not to take any chances."

"If Tomás's plans work out, it isn't going to matter what the mosquitoes do. Malaria isn't going to bother me if I'm dead." The words were said in a wryly philosophical tone that fell short of the mark. She sounded very young and very frightened and Ryder was infuriated by his urge to comfort her.

"You'll use the mosquito netting and, if I can lay my hands on some insect repellent, you'll use that too." The abruptness of the order revealed his own frustration.

She shrugged. "Sure. Until a mosquito or Tomás puts an end to my existence, what am I supposed to do? Am I expected to do something to earn my keep or do I just sit in here staring at the walls?"

"You're not expected to do anything but keep me entertained as long as you're here. I can't offer much by way of entertainment. There's the cards and I've got some books you can read." Cally glanced at him curiously. There was something in his tone that told her that this last offer was made grudgingly.

She'd heard it said that a lot could be learned about someone by looking at their choice of reading material. What would his books tell her about Ryder Allen?

He got to his feet. "The books are in my duffel bag. Help yourself. I'll be back in a few hours."

He ducked through the door, leaving her alone. She stared after him for a long time, her mind wandering from Ryder to her uncle to Tomás in a never-ending circle of speculation. Since her mother's death, Cally had been in control of her own life to a great extent. Her father had believed in letting his daughter have a say in any decision that related to her. She had grown up to be independent. But now she found herself in a situation where she had little or no say about what happened to her.

Her mouth tilted in a smile. Uncle Richard had always said that she was too independent for her own good. Maybe this would have a salutary effect. If she lived to appreciate it.

With a sigh, she got up and moved over to the duffel bag, tugging it over to the cot. Dwelling on the situation wasn't going to do her any good. At this point there was nothing she could do to change things. She was just going to have to try and keep her head clear and stay alert for anything that could work in her favor.

She unzipped the duffel bag and then hesitated. It seemed like an intrusion to go through Ryder's things, even though she had his permission. With a sigh, she closed the zipper. If the books had been right on top, it wouldn't have bothered her, but she didn't feel comfortable going through his things looking for them. She set the bag back where she'd found it and picked up the worn deck of cards. Nothing like retaining a nice sense of personal privacy in the middle of a terrorist camp in the middle of the Central American jungle.

The hours crawled by with a slowness that seemed cruelly deliberate. She played solitaire, inventing new rules as she went along. She ate a banana and then played yet more solitaire, feeling her nerves stretch tighter with each passing moment. It was getting harder and harder to remember that hysteria never did anybody any good.

She was just beginning to consider the possibility of ripping through the tent with her fingernails and running for the jungle when the sound of raised voices brought her upright on the cot. The hair on the back of her neck rose to attention as the voices came nearer. She looked around the tent frantically for something that could be used as a weapon but there was nothing.

Her fear subsided slightly when she heard the deeper tones of Ryder's voice mingling with the others. No matter what logic told her, she couldn't help but be reassured by his presence. She was on her feet, wiping her damp palms on the seat of her pants when the tent flap was thrust roughly inward and Ryder ducked through.

His face was hard, lines of tension bracketing the thick black mustache. "We've got trouble."

"What's wrong? Are they going to kill me?" Her voice rose on the question. One hand came out to clutch his forearm, the nails digging into his flesh. "Did he refuse to pay a ransom? Are they going to kill me?"

The quiver in her voice was like a knife in his heart. He could see her battling with her fear, trying to put up a brave front and he was touched despite himself. The unfamiliar emotion made his voice harder than he intended.

"There's no time to get hysterical. They're not going to kill you. Tomás wants to talk to you. Remember to think before you answer. Nobody's going to think it's strange if it takes you a while to pull an answer together. They're expecting you to be dazed." As he was speaking, he was brushing

56

lamp black over her cheek and jaw, re-creating the bruises of the night before. "I hope to God these will hold up in daylight," he muttered under his breath.

He wrapped his hand around her upper arm and pulled her roughly out of the tent, refusing to give in to the urge to reassure her any further.

Cally squeezed her eyes shut at the sudden brilliance of the sun. She had been in the filtered dimness of the tent for so long that it was like being under a spotlight. When she opened them again, the figures in front of her were slightly fuzzy around the edges.

Ryder stood beside her and she drew strength from his large presence, not even caring if it was false strength. His hand stayed around her arm and she was grateful for that, too. A dozen people stood in a half circle in front of the tent but she focused her attention on Tomás, who stood directly in front of her. The rest of the men would follow his lead. They were just there to provide an audience for whatever was about to happen.

Her stomach churned as she met Tomás's eyes and read the hostility in them. She swallowed hard and dropped her eyes. She didn't have to pretend to be afraid. She was terrified.

"We sent our demands to the capital today. To your father." The rushing in her ears made it difficult to follow Tomás's heavily accented English. "Do you know what we were told?"

She shook her head, too frightened to say a word.

"Your father has had a heart attack and is in the hospital, unable to be seen."

Uncle Richard? A heart attack? He was healthy as the proverbial horse. It just wasn't possible. She opened her mouth to say as much and then stopped as Ryder's fingers tightened around her arm. *Think before you answer.* As clearly as if he had shouted them in her ear, she heard the words again.

"Your father has a heart condition before?" As if compelled, her eyes lifted to meet Tomás's. Again, Ryder's hand tightened warningly.

"Y-yes. Yes, he's had a heart condition for a long time." The pressure around her arm eased and she could only hope it was because she'd come up with the right answer.

Tomás's eyes continued to bore into hers as if searching for the truth and Cally didn't have to fake the tears that rose to blur his face. She was so frightened. The only security in the world right now was represented by the man who stood so silently next to her and that was a shaky security at best.

She winced as Tomás's hand came up to grasp her right arm in a hold that duplicated Ryder's. But his fingers bit deep into her skin. He shook her slightly, leaning closer until mere inches separated his face from hers. Sour breath wafted across her face.

"If I should find that you are lying to me, señorita, or that your father is not really ill, you will be very sorry. I have men who know how to make dying take a *very* long time. *¿Comprende?*"

Cally nodded, her vivid imagination providing her with all sorts of unwelcome images.

Tomás released her and gestured sharply, spitting out several phrases too quick for Cally to follow. Ryder tugged on her arm and she followed him without question as he led her back into the tent. She was oblivious to the reluctant concern in his eyes. She sat down on the edge of the cot and hugged her arms around her body, rocking back and forth.

Outside the tent, Tomás continued to rage and, with a soft oath, Ryder ducked out, leaving Cally alone. *I am not going to fall to pieces. I am not going to fall to pieces.* She repeated the phrase over and over, struggling with the waves of panic that washed over her.

She didn't stir when Ryder stepped back into the tent. Ryder's eyes narrowed as he took in her hunched position and the way she rocked herself, like an infant seeking comfort. He came down in front of her, sitting back on his heels, putting their faces level.

"Cally?" His voice was gentle as he sought her attention. Her gaze was focused straight ahead and he was almost afraid of what he would find in her eyes when she blinked and slowly refocused on him. The clear gray was clouded with fear but underneath that was control. If panic flickered in the air, she was fighting it.

"Is he gone?"

"He's gone." He pulled her hands away from her arms. They were icy cold and he chafed them between his own broad palms, hardly conscious of the concern revealed in the gesture.

"I think I'm going to be sick."

"No, you're not. I don't allow people to be sick in here. The maid objects." The uncharacteristic jest surprised a weak smile out of Cally and Ryder was frightened by how much that smile meant to him. Who was Cally Stevens? She was symbolic of all he had given up. That was why he had this insane need to protect her. It was almost as if he were trying to protect the tattered remnants of old dreams.

"What happened to Uncle Richard? He's never been sick a day in his life. Did he really have a heart attack?" Her hands suddenly clutched at his. "Is he all right?"

"I don't know. I'm hoping he's just bought us some time."

Cally blinked. "You mean he may be faking the heart attack?" She lowered her voice to a whisper.

Ryder released her hands and pulled a cigarette out of his shirt pocket. "I don't know for sure but Richard Wellington didn't get where he is without being shrewd. What better way to buy time than to be unable to receive a ransom note?"

He lit the cigarette, inhaling deeply as he shifted to sit on the sleeping bag. He felt the need for that little bit of extra distance between them. He didn't like the things she did to his mind, the things she made him remember.

Cally nodded slowly, the fear receding from her eyes as she considered the possibilities. "Yes, it's possible. But what if he really is ill?"

"It serves the same purpose," he pointed out brutally. "It buys time. There's nothing you can do about it one way or the other so you might as well think positive."

Her mouth tilted up in a smile that quivered slightly around the edges. "I'd never have guessed that you were a closet optimist."

His smile was quick and gone almost as soon as it appeared. "Don't tell anybody. I'd hate to spoil my image." He glanced around the tent, taking in the cards which she had abandoned in a scattered heap. "Did you decide you didn't want to read?"

"I didn't want to go through your things. It seemed like an intrusion."

"Very admirable," he muttered dryly, stubbing out his cigarette. He grabbed the duffel bag and shifted it to lie beside him. He began emptying the bag, laying clothing in neat piles, separating out shaving gear and binoculars, odds and ends of tools, and several boxes of ammunition. Ammunition. Ammunition meant a gun. A gun might mean a way out of here.

"Don't even think about it," he said without looking up. Cally's heart jerked guiltily.

"Think about what?" Would the quiver in her voice betray her?

"A gun." He pulled several well-worn volumes from the bottom of the duffel bag before looking at her. She swallowed hard at the warning in his eyes.

"Even if you could find it, all it would do is get you killed. One gun isn't going to buy your way out of here."

Reluctantly, she acknowledged that he was right. "I suppose you're right. You can't blame me for thinking about it."

"You can think anything you like." He began packing things back into the duffel bag, his movements quick and economical. He'd forgotten about the ammunition when he told her to go through the bag and get out the books herself. *You're getting too old for this game when you begin to forget things. Time to get out while you're still alive.* He shook the thought away, a thought that was becoming all too common lately. He didn't know anything else. What was he going to "get out" and do? Sell insurance? Pump gas? He was too old and he'd been living in the cold for too long to set it aside and go back to living a life of quiet peace in the States.

It was just that he'd been on this job a long time and the strain was beginning to get to him. Soon this would be done and he'd go on to the next job. He shook his head, his mouth turning up in a rueful smile. No, he couldn't see himself getting a nine-to-five job and wearing a three-piece suit.

"I don't know if you'll—" He broke off as he lifted his head to find Cally curled up on the cot, her eyes closed, her breathing slow and even. With her hand tucked under her cheek, she looked like a child. But the feelings she aroused in him weren't childlike.

Her braid lay over her shoulder, the end of it trailing down past the edge of the cot. Without thinking, he reached out to grasp it. The end curled around his hand as if seeking to pull him closer. The pale gold was a brilliant contrast to the tanned skin of his forearm. One side of his mustache pulled down. Maybe the contrast was symbolic. She was certainly a creature of light. Perhaps after all these years of walking on the dark side, he had become too like those he stalked. Tainted by the elements he sought to destroy.

An angel and a devil. Her innocence and his . . . His what? A long time ago, he could have matched her, ideal for ideal. A very long time ago. Now he looked back on that younger, idealistic man as if looking the wrong way through a telescope. Small and far away, hard to remember.

He shook his head, laying the end of the braid over her shoulder. His hand seemed to tingle where the silvery coil had lain. He got to his feet and stood looking down at her, absently rubbing his thumb across that invisible mark. He had to get her out of here soon. For his own sake as well as hers. She was trouble for him.

When Cally awoke, she was disoriented for a moment. Not quite sure of where she was or what she was doing here. But the period of blissful ignorance was all too brief and she had the urge to close her eyes and court sleep again rather than face reality.

As she sat up, she reached for the canteen to

wash away the pastiness that made her feel as if her teeth were glued together. Without her watch there was no way to tell just how long she had slept, but her inner clock told her it hadn't been long.

She reached for a banana and peeled it slowly. Ryder was gone. She'd known that almost before she'd known she was awake. She chewed thoughtfully on a bite of fruit. Ryder was going to help her. It didn't matter how many times she told herself she couldn't count on that, something inside kept insisting that she trust him. Gut instinct or psychic flash or sheer desperation. Whatever it was, she was going to go with it.

Ryder would probably be appalled if he could read her thoughts. She smiled, feeling her sense of humor stir cautiously. She knew that the last thing Ryder Allen wanted was to be saddled with her trust. It was bad enough that he was saddled with her. Well, what he didn't know wouldn't bother him, she decided, feeling almost cheerful.

Her eyes fell on the half a dozen paperbacks stacked neatly next to the crate. She picked them up, shuffling through them curiously. Her brows rose as she read the titles. Plutarch's *Lives*. The works of Plato in Greek. The *Rubáiyát* in English. Chaucer's *Canterbury Tales* in the original Middle English. A reference book of quotations and a battered novel by John le Carré.

She ran her thumb over the spine of the Chaucer, intrigued by the eclectic blend of reading material. A strange man. Terrorist or spy, he was not easy to pigeonhole. He spoke Spanish as if it were his first language. He had books in Greek and Middle English. Poetry, philosophy, classics, and a modern novel. She shook her head. If she had hoped that she'd be able to learn something about him from his choice of reading matter, she was doomed to disappointment. It just presented her with more questions than she'd had to start with. At least he provided her with something more to think about than whether or not she was going to be alive the next day.

CHAPTER FOUR

By the next morning, Cally felt as if the entire world had shrunk until it held nothing beyond the walls of the tent. The noises outside the canvas walls were hard to connect to other people because it was difficult to remember that other people existed.

The only break in the monotony came when Ryder stepped into her small world, shattering the torpor that threatened to consume her. His presence brought the real world into sharp focus, reminding her that there was a world outside. But not one she wanted to be part of.

When she woke soon after dawn, it was hard to realize that only forty-eight hours ago she had awakened in a luxurious hotel suite thinking that the only danger in her immediate future was a bumpy jeep ride into the country's interior. She lay on the cot staring up at the ceiling of the tent, refusing to do more than open her eyes. Maybe if she didn't move, this would all fade away and she'd be back in the suite, waiting for her uncle to wake up and tell her what his plans were.

But it didn't fade away and, with a muffled sigh, she sat up, swinging her legs over the side of the cot. Her back twinged a sullen protest at the movement, complaining about the quality of the bed, but Cally ignored the mild discomfort. A sore back was the least of her worries.

Ryder was gone, the sleeping bag was neatly rolled and set against a wall. A wave of loneliness threatened to sweep over her. He was her lifeline. She might have doubts about the eventual outcome of his companionship but, for now, he was all she had and she had never been one to look a gift horse in the mouth.

Cally stretched, rubbing her hand over her face and grimacing at the sticky feel of her skin. If she made it back to civilization in one piece, she was going to take a long, hot bath and give thanks for the wonders of modern plumbing.

There was a banana and a mango lying on the crate and the usual plate of tortillas. Lethargically, she reached out to pick up a tortilla, rolling it into a tube before biting into the chewy dough. Two days. How many more days lay ahead with nothing to do but read and play solitaire and wonder just when Tomás was going to get tired of feeding her? How many more days before the strain got to her and she went stark, raving mad?

She couldn't afford to think like that. She had to hold on to the belief that she was going to get out of this. Somehow, she was going to make it through. Whether it was logical or not, she had to believe that Ryder would help her; that he would get her out alive. She couldn't afford to believe anything else. He was all she had.

She forced herself to comb her hair and braid it neatly, trying not to notice the film of dirt that dulled the gold of it. She tipped water onto the hem of her shirt and used it to wipe her face, trying to convince herself that she felt refreshed by the tepid moisture.

When Ryder ducked into the tent two hours later, Cally was sitting cross-legged on the cot, the worn cards spread out in a game of solitary concentration as she tried to match pairs. She looked up and smiled at him, feeling as if her facial muscles might split apart from the strain of the movement.

His eyes sharpened, taking in the trapped look hovering at the back of her gaze, the panic that threatened to break through her control. She'd done remarkably well, all things considered. The pressure that she'd been under would have been enough to break a lot of people and she'd managed to hold it together. But he didn't need a degree in psychology to see that her control was cracking.

"I don't seem to be doing too well at concentration today." She gestured to the cards and he could see the fine tremor in her fingers. "Ridiculous really. I don't have anything to do but concentrate."

"I've got some good news for you."

"I could sure use some."

"I've gotten permission for you to use Elena's bathroom. It's the only semi-civilized facility around. It's not the Marriott but it's a lot better than the communal latrine."

The words worked like magic. All her depression vanished in a flash. The only thing that could have made her happier was an announcement that the marines had just blasted their way into the camp and were waiting outside to escort her home. Cally was tugging on her shoes before he'd finished speaking.

"I take it you're interested in the offer?" She glanced up from tying her shoes and caught a glimpse of humor lighting the blue of his eyes.

"Right now, I'd probably kill for a chance at a real bathroom. Will I be able to wash up?"

"I don't think Elena would mind. She's got her quirks but she's generally too lazy to cause trouble."

If Cally had hoped that seeing the camp in daylight would give her more hope for escape, she was disappointed. With Ryder's hand wrapped around her upper arm in a grip designed to look forceful and painful but actually very reassuring, she walked across the dusty area enclosed by the huts and tents and felt her spirits sink still lower.

In daylight, she could see, not only the wall of brush that guarded the camp, but the jungle outside that wall. Green on green, she knew that the foliage would be so dense that it was almost impossible to see the separate parts. Tree ferns, matapalo, orchids and mosses and more varieties of plant and insect life than existed anywhere else on earth. She had been in enough jungles with her father to know their beauty. But it was a beauty that could kill. If you didn't know the terrain, it was all too easy to get lost forever in those lush depths.

This was Central America and there were no neatly uniformed forest rangers to come to the rescue. Once inside that wall of greenery, she would be on her own. And, with no knowledge of the area, without so much as a compass for guidance, she would be little better off than she was here, waiting for Tomás to hand down a death sentence.

Her footsteps wavered slightly and she felt rather than saw Ryder's questioning glance. With an effort, she forced herself to concentrate on the present. As they neared the sagging building at one end of the rough circle of the camp, Cally became aware that they were the center of attention. Or rather, *she* was the center of attention. All around them, the camp was still and quiet. Except for the scrawny dogs who lay sprawled in the morning sun, every eye was turned to follow their progress.

She fought the urge to break into a tap dance routine or fall to her knees and burst into song; something to justify their interest. There was more than a touch of hysteria in the thought and she swallowed it down. She kept her eyes lowered, stealing sidelong glances.

It was mostly women and children who stood outside their huts and stared at this stranger in their midst. The men who were visible seemed to make it a point to show their indifference, though she had the feeling that their interest was just as keen.

The silent staring was eerie and her shoulders jerked slightly as a convulsive shiver worked its way up her spine.

Ryder must have sensed her discomfort because his hand tightened on her arm, drawing her closer to his side as he lengthened his stride slightly. "Don't let it get to you. We don't often get strangers in camp, let alone a blond woman."

Staying with her role as terrified captive was remarkably easy under these circumstances and Cally said nothing, quickening her pace to match his without complaint. Even the company of the sullen Elena was preferable to this.

The interior of the house was dim, giving the illusion of being cool, though the temperature inside was a close match for the ninety-degree weather outside. The clear light of day was not as kind as the lanterns had been and every crack, every inch of peeling paint showed with unpleasant clarity.

"Elena is probably still in bed. She makes it a point to sleep until at least noon." Cally had to suppress the urge to ask how he knew. "The bathroom is through that door. I'll be back in half an hour." He turned to go and then stopped and turned back to her. "Don't do anything stupid, like try to go out a window. If, by some chance, the guards missed shooting you, you'd never survive the jungle."

He was gone before she could think of a reply.

Cally stared after him for a moment and then shrugged and crossed the room to the battered door he had indicated. There was no sense trying to fathom Ryder Allen. For now, she was just going to have to take life *and* him one step at a time. And the first step was to get clean.

There was no lock on the door and she hesitated for a long moment before shrugging. Elena was asleep and Tomás was gone. And even if Tomás were here, he wouldn't risk Elena finding him with another woman. She had half an hour and she was going to make the most of it.

She quickly stripped off Ryder's shirt and her jeans and underwear and wrapped a towel around her body. Maybe no one was around but she felt better with something covering her. She rinsed her bra and panties in the sink, hanging them over the rust-pitted towel rod to dry. It wasn't easy, but by bending her neck at an impossible angle, she managed to get her head under the faucet to wash her hair. She sighed with pleasure as the tepid water washed away the dirt of the past forty-eight hours.

With her clean hair wrapped in one of the towels, she turned her attention to the grime that was ground into her skin. Using a thin washcloth and a sliver of soap that had been lurking unhappily behind the faucet, she soaped up the rag and began to scrub briskly, starting with her face and working her way down. With every centimeter cleaned, she felt a little better, as if she were actually washing away the fear along with the dirt.

She was just rinsing the last inch of bare foot

when the door to the bathroom opened without warning. Cally jerked upright, barely missing the sink with her head, her hands automatically clutching the towel tighter around her breasts. She felt horribly vulnerable. If it was Tomás . . .

Elena stopped in the doorway, her voluptuous figure encased in a robe of scarlet satin in a style that would have made Jean Harlow envious. Her heavy breasts were barely covered by the turned-back lapels, and the belt that was carelessly tied at the waist looked as if it might slip loose at any moment. Cally would have looked like a little girl playing dress-up but Elena looked magnificently sensual and decadent and all woman.

"Hello. I had not remembered that you were to be here." The words were mumbled around a sleepy yawn as the other woman thrust her fingers through the heavy mane of hair that straggled down the back of the robe.

"That's okay. I was almost done. I . . . I appreciate you letting me use your bathroom."

"De nada." Elena scratched absently at a bug bite, her dark eyes going over Cally's near-naked figure more carefully than they had the night before and coming to the same conclusion. No competition.

She showed no sign of moving from her casual pose against the door jamb and Cally realized that her privacy was at an end. With a mental sigh, she picked up her panties and struggled to pull them on without losing her grip on the towel. The fabric was still slightly damp and resisted her efforts but persistence won out in the end. She had no choice but to turn her back and drop the towel to put on her bra and she could feel Elena studying her every minute. Not in a malicious way but as if she had never seen a creature quite like Cally before and she found her mildly interesting.

"Your hair is a strange color."

Cally pushed the damp weight of it back from her face, wishing she'd left it wrapped in the towel. She finally managed to hook her bra and grabbed up Ryder's shirt. "My father always call . . . calls it silver but it has some gold in the sunlight." Just in time, she managed to change the tense. She had to remember who Elena thought she was. With the shirt buttoned, it covered her modestly from throat to almost knees and she felt less exposed.

"Your hair is very lovely," she told the other woman sincerely.

"Gracias." The compliment was accepted with a regal nod as if acknowledging a well-known fact. Cally bit the inside of her lip and reached for her jeans.

"You wear Rico's shirt, no?"

"My own was ruined." She confined her answer to that. She snapped the waist of her jeans and sat down on the edge of the cracked enamel tub to pull on her socks and the lightweight boots she had worn in anticipation of hiking to the archaeological site.

"Rico is much a man." Elena scratched absently

at a bite, letting the robe fall open, revealing a length of unwashed leg.

"Mmm," Cally mumbled as she tied the laces on one boot. What was she supposed to say to that? The man had supposedly raped her. Did Elena expect Cally to praise his manly physique?

"I have Tomás, of course, but a woman notices a man like that."

How long did she have to wait before Ryder came back for her? She reached for the other boot and pulled it on slowly, taking her time. As long as she had something else to do, maybe Elena wouldn't expect her to say anything coherent. But there was only so long that putting on a shoe could be drawn out.

She stood up, letting her eyes meet Elena's. There was a shrewd intelligence there that surprised her, cracking the image of slovenly decadence. She flinched as the other woman reached out to flick her fingers lightly against Cally's cheekbone.

"Your bruises fade quickly."

Cally's hand flew to her face. Ryder had carefully applied the lamp black to her face again this morning and she had just as carefully scrubbed it off. Her wide eyes met Elena's and her mouth opened but no words came out. What could she say?

"Men." Elena flicked her fingers contemptuously. "They are so foolish."

"Er . . . yes, aren't they?" Cally's head was beginning to ache with the effort of following this obscure conversation. Was Elena going to tell Tomás about the bruises? "He . . . he . . ."

"You do not have to tell me. He did not want Tomás to think he had been too kind." Again, that contemptuous little gesture that expressed so much. "Men must play their stupid little games." Cally nodded, grateful for the explanation Elena had handed her.

The other woman eyed her speculatively. "You are very thin and pale. Does Rico find you attractive?"

Where are you, Ryder? "I . . . I don't know."

"But he takes you, yes? He must desire you." Her tone was curious and slightly puzzled and Cally wasn't sure how to respond. Did this woman really expect her to be pleased at what Ryder was supposed to have done? But then, all Elena saw was the lack of bruises. To her, maybe that indicated that Cally couldn't have too many complaints.

She was saved from finding an answer by the creak of the screen door. Please God, let it be Ryder. If it was Tomás and he noticed the lack of bruises . . . Elena turned and Cally caught her sultry smile in profile before the other woman stepped away from the door.

"Rico. This is twice that I have seen you in a short while."

"Elena." Ryder gave her a half smile, ignoring the way her hands reached up to straighten his collar. She leaned into him with the movement, letting her breasts brush across his chest and he met her eyes, reading the open invitation. He was never quite sure just how serious that invitation was. There had been a time when he was tempted to find out but now her dark beauty looked over-blown and gaudy and the heavy musk perfume she wore made his head ache.

He looked over her head to where Cally stood in the bathroom door. His brows came together, creating a thick black line across his forehead. She was so pale. What had Elena said to her? She gave a shaky smile that did little to reassure.

Cally took a deep breath, trying to steady her knees. She was vaguely aware of Elena talking to Ryder and equally aware of his lukewarm response to the other woman. For some reason, that realization pleased her.

His eyes were searching as he stepped forward to wrap his hand around her upper arm. She was aware of Elena's dark eyes studying them and she searched her mind for the right response. Did Elena expect her to throw herself at Ryder?

"Hello." Her voice was husky with strain. She dropped her eyes to the floor, missing the sharpened look in his.

"I have just been telling Lisa that she is fortunate that it was you who claimed her, Rico, rather than some of the pigs that claim allegiance to my husband."

He didn't even try to find an answer to her dubious compliment. "I'm sure Lisa appreciates your generosity in letting her use your facilities."

Elena's shrug covered Cally's murmured thanks.

"De nada. She is not a *puta* like the other women. I do not mind having her in my house."

As Ryder led her out into the hot sunshine, Cally could feel Elena's eyes following them and she wondered what the other woman was thinking. Clearly, Elena's lethargic exterior covered a mind that was not at all lethargic. She would have to be careful around her.

Cally wouldn't have believed that she could actually be grateful to be back within the confines of the tent. When she'd awakened this morning to feel the walls closing in on her, she'd thought that nothing could make her happier than to get out. But after Elena's dubious companionship and running the gantlet of eyes as Ryder led her back through camp, it felt almost like coming home to step into the dim heat of the tent.

"I'll take you back over this afternoon. Will you be okay until then?"

Cally turned to look at him, wondering how he'd come to represent security to her when, for all she knew, he might present dangers all his own.

"Sure. Ryder." She stopped him when he would have left but, when he turned back, his brow raised in question, she wasn't quite sure what to say to him. She didn't want to be alone again. When she was alone, she had too much time to think. But she couldn't ask him to stay.

"I didn't know that Elena and Tomás were married." It was a weak excuse to keep him there but she didn't care.

"Only by common law. Elena likes to refer to

him as her husband, Tomás likes to refer to her as his woman. She doesn't call him husband when he might hear her and he doesn't call her mistress when she might hear him. I don't know if they're really fooling each other or if it's a game they play."

He turned to leave and Cally found herself stopping him again. "Will you be far away?" There was a quiver in her voice that she despised but she was helpless to prevent it. She was terrified by the thought that he might leave her without protection.

For just an instant, his eyes softened. "I won't be far. We each take a turn at guard duty. It's part of our fearless leader's master plan toward equality for all."

The dry humor in his voice drew a smile from her. "Naturally, his other responsibilities prevent him from taking part in many of these duties."

"Naturally." He smiled as their eyes met. The smile faded as he looked at her and Cally wondered what it was he saw that caused his mouth to tighten. "I'll be back later."

He turned and ducked through the tent opening. Cally stared at the blank panel for a moment, willing Ryder's large, reassuring form to return. The more time she spent alone in this small enclosure, the harder it was to watch him leave. She couldn't depend on him for everything, she told herself sternly. Emotionally, she had to rely on only herself. The brief pep talk did little to cheer her and her movements were limp as she sat down on the edge of the cot and reached for the comb. If she took her time, she would be able to kill the better part of an hour just getting the tangles out of her hair.

Ryder returned before she had even half the job done. He'd forgotten his matches, he told her. Half an hour later, Cally was trying to lose herself in the John le Carré novel when he came back and said that he was out of cigarettes. Forty-five minutes after that, he brought her lunch. Then he came back to make sure she had enough water. Half an hour went by and he was there to take her to Elena's house to use the bathroom.

At the end of the day, she realized that he had made it a point to check in on her at least every hour. She was touched by the gesture but she knew better than to thank him for it. It didn't take a genius to figure out that he wouldn't appreciate her thanks.

Dinner that night was a plate of chicken and vegetable stew. The vegetables were plentiful, though not always identifiable but, if a chicken had ever been near the stew, he had merely walked through the vegetables and went on his merry way. The food was not unpleasant and it was filling, and most important, Ryder stayed in the tent to eat his own meal. They didn't talk much but it didn't matter. Just having him there made the food taste much better than it really was.

She dragged out the meal as long as possible, afraid that once the food was gone, Ryder would leave. But, eventually, she had mopped up the last of the thin gravy with a piece of tortilla and she couldn't pretend any more interest in the empty plate. Ryder lounged on the floor, the rolled sleeping bag providing a prop for his back as he smoked a cigarette, his eyes focused somewhere past her. He must have been aware of her though. As soon as she set her plate down, he picked it up and stacked it on top of his.

"Are you going to be gone for long?" The question popped out almost before it formed in her mind. He turned to look at her and she bit the inside of her lip, trying to look as if the answer were only of minor interest.

"I'm just going to get some hot water so I can shave." It wasn't at all what he had intended to do. He'd planned on leaving her alone until he was reasonably certain she had fallen asleep. But, sitting there in the golden gleam of the lamplight, she looked so small and so frightened. His fingers tightened on the plates as he watched relief flood her eyes. With a mental curse, he turned and ducked through the doorway, wishing he'd never heard of Cally Stevens.

Cally felt amazingly lighthearted as she watched him prepare to shave. Logical or not, there was comfort in his large presence.

Ryder's eyes narrowed on the cracked mirror that he'd propped on the old packing crate. He was uncomfortably aware of her eyes on him and he gave serious thought to the idea of just letting his beard grow. He wasn't accustomed to having someone watching him. He slathered shaving soap over his face using an old-fashioned brush, letting the lather soften his beard and trying to pretend that he didn't have an audience.

He picked up the straight razor and ran it carefully down the side of his face. There was a flicker of movement in the mirror and his eyes shifted to see Cally behind him, unconsciously twisting her mouth to the side in imitation of him. A sharp stab of pain brought his attention back to the task at hand but it was too late. A thin trickle of blood mingled with the lather on his chin, turning it pale pink. His brows hooked together in a scowl. Ignoring the small cut, he rinsed off the blade and started on the next section of bristly skin. This time, he was going to ignore his audience.

The blade had barely traversed half the length of his jaw when he found himself watching Cally again. This time, her gray eyes were wide and her teeth nibbled at her lower lip. She looked like she expected him to slash an artery at any moment. Distracted, he promptly proved that her fears were not unjustified.

"Damn it!" He set the razor down and picked up a rag to dab at the new cut. His scowl deepened. Much more of this and he was going to bleed to death before the night was over.

"You know, I used to shave my dad." Cally's voice was hesitant, the offer unspoken.

Ryder turned to look at her, his eyes shooting blue sparks. He had been shaving himself since he was sixteen and he didn't need anybody to do it for him. Certainly not a girl who was barely old enough to be let out at night.

But her eyes were so hopeful and eager. She made him remember the first time his father had let him take the car out without an adult to supervise.

"Your father didn't die of a slashed throat, did he?"

Cally's eyes widened. "He was killed when a tunnel collapsed. Why?"

"Then I suppose it would be safe to let you shave me." She blinked, trying to make the connection and then a soft gurgle of laughter bubbled out.

"Daddy never had any complaints. Sit down here so I can reach your face." Ryder let her push him down onto the cot and tried not to let his misgivings show as she picked up the razor and turned toward him. "Turn your face to the light and do this." His eyes gleamed with laughter but he obediently twisted his face in the direction she indicated. He was so busy watching her intent expression that he forgot to wince when she set the blade to his face.

"I only cut Daddy once, actually." She wiped the blade and returned for another stroke. "Of course, it *was* ten stitches and he never looked quite the same."

With the blade against his jaw, Ryder didn't dare move but his eyes widened expressively. Cally met the look and grinned. "I'm kidding. My father's face never suffered any damage from me."

"Sadist," he muttered as she wiped the blade again.

"I know."

Ryder found himself watching her face, enjoying the way her mouth twisted to match the movement of his. Her movements were smooth and he slowly relaxed, letting the slow stroke of the blade set the rhythm for his thoughts. Her hands were soft as she tilted his head in the direction she wanted and he found himself wondering what they would feel like on his body.

His eyes narrowed on the heavy braid of hair that swung over her shoulder as she worked. It wasn't hard to picture that silver-gold fall spread out across a pillow. Would her eyes go stormy gray with passion? Would her nails dig into the muscles of his back?

Arousal was hot in his veins and he shut his eyes, willing his body to relax, willing his mind to go blank. Her breast brushed against his shoulder as she leaned forward and he fought the urge to sweep her to him, to pin her beneath him on the cot and bury his aching arousal in her sweet warmth.

"You certainly look a lot more respectable."

Cally's bright voice shattered his thoughts and Ryder opened his eyes slowly, hoping the lamplight was too dim to allow her to read his expression. She held up the cracked mirror and he forced himself to look in it. The face that looked back at him was hard-edged, even without the scruffy growth of beard. Respectable? You had only to look into his eyes to know that respectable was not a word that could be applied to him. Not for more years than he cared to count.

"Thanks."

Cally's smile widened and he found himself wishing that he could give her more to smile about. His mouth tightened as he used a rag to wipe the last of the shaving soap from his face and stood up.

"I'll toss this water out and then we'd better get to bed."

Lying in the dark a few minutes later, Cally stared up at the black ceiling and wondered if Ryder had been as unaffected by her nearness as he had seemed. She rubbed her fingers together, trying to erase the warmth that seemed to linger from his skin. She didn't like the way that tingle had spread through her body. It was one thing to give him her tentative trust. It was something else altogether to become attracted to him.

She shut her eyes, willing her mind to go blank. At least in sleep, she wouldn't have to deal with all the confusing thoughts that were spinning in her head. Too bad she couldn't just sleep her way through this whole nightmare.

CHAPTER FIVE

Cally slid the needle in and out of the garish purple fabric in a smooth rhythm. It had been years since she'd done any sewing but it hadn't taken long for her mother's lessons to come back. There was something soothing about the smooth pattern of sliding the needle in and out.

Across from her, Elena sat in an overstuffed chair that had once been upholstered in a heavy brocade. The fabric was so old that only traces of the pattern could be seen and Cally marveled that the springs had not yet broken through the worn fibers. A spill of bright green satin lay in Elena's lap but her hands were occupied with more interesting things than repairing torn hems. On a rickety little table next to her chair sat a box of chocolates. They had melted slightly during the trip from the capital but that didn't bother Elena.

She ate them at a steady pace that Cally could only marvel at. Her hand moved from box to mouth without any apparent pause to chew. Periodically, the rhythm was broken by her wiping her fingers on a lace-edged handkerchief that lay on the arm of the chair. The fact that she sometimes missed the hankie and wiped chocolate on the chair didn't seem to bother her in the least.

Over the past four days, Cally had developed a certain respect for Elena. She had never met anyone quite so wholly self-centered as Elena and the experience fascinated her. Shut away in this tumbledown shack, surrounded by Elena's own peculiar brand of luxury, it was almost possible to forget her true position here.

"Tomás grows impatient with your father's illness."

Cally's hand slipped and she sucked in a quick breath as the needle jabbed her finger. She lifted her hand to her mouth and sucked on the tiny wound, tasting the metallic tang of blood. It seemed appropriate to the moment.

"I just hope my father is going to be all right."

"Tomás does not like to be kept waiting." Elena downed another chocolate, her heavy-lidded eyes focused on her companion with distant curiosity.

"Well, I'm certain my father didn't plan on having a heart attack." Cally kept her gaze on the skirt, willing her fingers not to shake.

"Perhaps." Elena licked her fingers before wiping them, this time on the front of the black satin robe she was wearing. "Rico has been treating you well, yes?"

Apparently, the subject of Tomás's lack of patience had been exhausted and Cally didn't dare to probe further. She might not like the answers she came up with. She shrugged. Ryder was a favorite topic of Elena's and she was never quite sure what reaction the other woman expected from her.

"Rico is *muy macho*. Many of the women have offered to keep his bed warm at night. *Putas.*" She spit out the word with casual contempt and Cally swallowed the urge to smile. Sitting there, in her worn satin robe, her hair a tangled mass on her back, eyes heavily lined in black, Elena was the very image of a cheap slut, but she obviously considered herself several cuts above the other women in the camp. Cally's mouth quirked. Who knows? Maybe she was right. Her attitude had served to cut her off from female companionship but Cally doubted if she'd missed it much. Elena was very much a man's woman.

"Many women have wanted Rico but he holds himself much apart." She reached for another chocolate and bit into it with absent pleasure. "If I did not have Tomás, I myself might have been tempted to allow him into my bed."

Cally raised one brow, her head still bent over the sewing. She had the feeling that, Tomás or no, if Ryder had shown any interest, Elena would not have protested. She continued to sew, aware of the other woman finishing the first layer of chocolates and starting on the second.

"Tomás says that Rico claimed you in front of the men."

Cally lifted her shoulders again, wishing that she could think of some better reaction to Elena's constant probing.

"He must have wanted you very much."

Elena's tone made it clear that she found this amazing. She obviously saw nothing in Cally that would appeal to a man, especially not when he could have had Elena herself. Luckily, Elena seemed to find this more of a curiosity than an insult.

"Has Rico been here long?" The question popped out without Cally really thinking about it. She knew so little about Ryder.

Elena shrugged, a magnificent gesture that slid one side of the robe down her arm. "Not quite a year. Tomás was not quite sure about having a norteamericano with us but Rico brought useful information. He does not talk much about himself. At first, the men wanted to challenge him, to make him prove his worth."

She stopped to pop a chocolate into her mouth, chewing slowly, leaving Cally hanging on her words. She bit her tongue to prevent herself from urging the other woman to continue. After a long moment, Elena swallowed and went on.

"He is very skilled with that knife he wears. The men soon learned to leave him alone."

A shiver ran up Cally's spine. Elena didn't have to go into details. She could imagine what must have happened. Still, better to have Ryder and his knife on her side than on Tomás's. If only she could be certain that it was on her side.

Elena fell silent, apparently exhausted by her conversational efforts, and Cally continued to sew. After a week in Tomás's camp, she had come to the conclusion that if she was going to make it out of here alive, she was going to do it because Ryder got her out. Tomás might be a nasty little braggart but he was not careless. The only way she was getting out of this camp without Ryder was if they carried her out in a box. She kept her eyes open, trying to be alert for any opportunity, but her hopes rested with Ryder. And, whatever hand he was playing, he was keeping it very close to his chest.

She bit off a thread and rethreaded the needle. Across from her, Elena's eyes were closed and she had no idea whether the woman slept or just didn't want to talk. Elena had, in her own way, been kind. The use of the primitive bathroom in the cottage went a long way toward keeping Cally sane, and she was grateful. She didn't mind making repairs on Elena's clothes. At least it got her out of the tent.

There was a brief knock on the outer door and then the warped screen door squealed and heavy boots crossed the floor. Cally set down her sewing, trying to ignore the disturbing tightness in her chest. It was Ryder. She recognized his footsteps. She felt flushed and she took a deep breath, forcing herself to look away from the door. Her eyes met Elena's and she was disturbed by the knowing look in the woman's dark eyes.

"Time to go." Cally's gaze shifted back to the doorway and she tried not to notice how his broad shoulders filled the doorway, or the way the battered hat shadowed his face. She set everything aside neatly and got to her feet, smoothing her palms over her thighs.

"I'll see you tomorrow, Elena."

Elena nodded without shifting her eyes from Ryder. She crossed her legs, letting the black satin fall back to expose her naked legs. Of course, in Cally's opinion, the unshaven length of leg was not particularly attractive but perhaps Ryder felt differently. If he did, she couldn't tell it. Not by so much as a blink did he reveal any awareness of the invitation implicit in Elena's gesture.

He wrapped his fingers around Cally's arm and nodded to Elena.

Outside, the air was hot and humid. They were in for rain. It didn't take an expert to predict that much. The weather had been unseasonably dry over the past week but it was going to break soon. If not this afternoon, then tomorrow. Perhaps a storm would ease some of the tension that simmered in the air.

Ryder strode beside her silently, not speaking even when they ducked into the tent. Usually, he returned her to the tent and then left again but, this time, he tossed his hat onto the cot and settled down in the folding chair. Cally sat on the cot.

She waited for him to say something but he remained silent, his eyes fixed blankly ahead of him. The stillness inside was so complete that she jumped when a dog barked somewhere nearby. Ryder didn't seem to notice. He reached for his cigarettes and lit one. She twisted her braid around her fingers, stealing quick glances at him. He was obviously very unhappy about something. His mouth was set in tight lines and a muscle worked along his jaw, knotting and unknotting as if he were chewing on some problem.

"Is something wrong?" For a moment, she thought he hadn't heard the question. He didn't move, didn't even blink. When his voice finally came, it was a low rasp with frustration edging the words.

"Why the hell didn't you listen to Wellington and stay out of Central America?"

Cally blinked at the unexpected attack. "What?"

His eyes shifted, snapping into focus on her and she winced back at the anger that seemed to turn his eyes to cobalt.

"Do you know how long I've been working on this? Ten and half lousy months. Ten and a half months of putting up with Tomás, treating him like he was a general instead of the two-bit hoodlum he is. Ten and half months and I was so close. So close and you're going to destroy it all."

"It's not my fault Tomás kidnapped me." Cally wasn't sure if it was indignation or tears that put a quiver in her voice. Perhaps a little of both.

"If you'd listened to reason and stayed in the States, Tomás wouldn't have had a chance to kidnap you. Almost a year of my life wasted because you were too goddamned spoiled to stay home."

"I didn't ask you to help me." She sniffed back tears and tried not to think of what was going to happen to her if he turned his back on her now.

"I'm sorry if my being here has messed you up but it's hardly my fault."

"No?"

"No! I don't want to be here any more than you want me here."

"Then why didn't you listen to Wellington?" The question was unanswerable. Uncle Richard *had* told her not to come. "You didn't listen because you're spoiled and stubborn. Maybe you can get away with that in the States. But this time, it just might get you killed. You and me both."

He surged to his feet and stalked out of the tent before Cally could think of anything to say. She stood up and took two quick steps before catching herself. She might want to chase after him and argue against his accusations but it wouldn't be a smart thing to do. He might think she was spoiled but she wasn't stupid.

She paced around the tent—a frustrating exercise because the space was so limited. Finally she plopped down on the cot and stared into space, her fingers twisting restlessly around her braid. It wasn't fair. How could he blame her for getting kidnapped? She hadn't gone out looking for Tomás. She hadn't worn a sign that announced that she was a worthy target for kidnapping.

But she hadn't been as careful as she should have been. She tried to ignore the little voice but it was insistent. She *should* have listened when Uncle Richard told her it wasn't safe for her to come with him. She should have spent more time checking the credentials of her guides. She should have done a lot of things that she hadn't. Maybe there was some justification for Ryder's anger.

She picked up his hat and twisted it round and round in her fingers. The fabric was a dusty brown, worn with time and use. She rubbed her thumb over the aged surface, wondering what the plain headwear would tell her about Ryder Allen if it could talk. Would it say that she was foolish to put so much faith in him?

Ryder thrust his fingers through his hair. He'd left the tent without his hat. The realization brought a muttered curse. It was barely a week since Cally Stevens had been thrown into his life and she had already managed to disrupt old habits. He lifted his hand in a vague salute to the guard as he stepped through the gate. A few yards outside the gate and he was in the jungle, greenery closing around him, shutting off the rest of the world.

He stopped and took a slow drag on his cigarette. There were times when he wanted to just walk into the jungle and keep walking until he'd left everything and everyone behind. He shook his head and crushed the cigarette out. He pocketed the butt automatically. Cigarette butts were as good as a neon sign in pointing out where a man had been.

He inhaled sharply, smelling the damp, half rotten smell that was so typical of the jungle that he barely noticed it anymore. He looked around but he didn't see the exotic beauty of the plant life that pressed in on him. Instead, he saw a pair of gray eyes, wet with tears and dark with fright. He shouldn't have taken his frustrations out on her. The thought slipped in unwanted. It wasn't her fault that Tomás was uncooperative. And it wasn't her fault that her presence threatened everything he'd been working toward.

He shoved one hand in the pocket of his khaki safari pants. Around him the jungle murmured with life. Unseen birds called from one tree to another. Soft scuttling noises indicated animal life that was hidden from the casual intruder like himself. If he was honest about it, he wasn't angry over Tomás's refusal to take him into his confidence. That was to be expected. He wasn't even really angry that Cally's arrival had thrown such a monkey wrench into his plans.

His shoulders twitched beneath the dusty gray shirt. It was the things she made him remember that angered him. It had been so long since he'd thought of his family, wondered what they were doing with their lives. He hadn't been home in almost ten years, hadn't written in five. He'd long ago come to terms with the fact that he couldn't keep a foot in both worlds. He'd seen too much and done too much to ever settle into a cozy suburban setting with a wife and two kids and a station wagon. He'd accepted that and he'd never allowed himself to regret the decision.

He couldn't even remember the last time he'd consciously thought of his family. He knew he'd be informed if anything happened to his parents or his brother and sister and he was content to leave it that way.

But Cally suddenly brought all kinds of things to mind. Things he'd thought forgotten. She made him remember the taste of his mother's fried chicken, the way grass smelled as it was being cut, and the scent of wood shavings as he smoothed a wood plane over a sturdy plank.

He realized that his hands were clenched and he forced them open, looking down at his palms. His hands were a lot more accustomed to holding a gun or a machete than they were to holding tools. He shook his head. He'd chosen this path a long time ago and there was no going back now. He'd just go on from one assignment to another. Until they forced him to retire or he lost the edge that had kept him alive this long.

He wiped a trickle of sweat from his forehead. It was just the heat. Next time, he'd see if they could give him something in a climate that didn't resemble hell's back door. He reached up to tug down the brim of his hat, muttering a curse as his fingers grasped air. She'd made him forget the damn thing. But there was no anger in the thought.

Cally scanned the first line of the page but it didn't register this time any more than it had the last six or seven times she'd read it. Her ears were tuned to any sound that might indicate that Ryder was returning. What if he didn't come back? He had to come back. After all, this was his tent. But what if he didn't? She refused to even consider the possibility, turning her attention firmly back to the page. But not even John le Carré could distract her. It was impossible to become absorbed in a fictional adventure when she was right in the midst of a real one.

For all her tension, Cally was unprepared when Ryder ducked through the entrance of the tent. She had planned to have a speech all made up, apologizing for any problems she'd caused him. It didn't matter that it wasn't by her choice that she was causing him problems. She couldn't afford to have him angry with her and she'd swallow her pride and placate him if she could.

But the moment he was standing in front of her, everything she'd planned to say flew out of her head and she could only stare at him, trying to think of something intelligent to say. He looked as uncomfortable as she felt, though it was hard to read much expression in those impassive features.

His eyes met hers and then shifted away and he tugged on the end of his mustache with one hand. In the other hand he held a straw hat with a wide brim.

"I . . . ah . . . thought it would be a good idea if you had a hat." His voice was huskier than usual, another sign of discomfort. He looked at the hat he held as if trying to remember how it came to be there and then held it out to her.

Cally smiled, blinking quickly to hold back the tears that threatened. She took the hat from him with a murmur of thanks. The straw felt cool in her fingers. Cool and silky. She ran her fingertips along the brim, testing the weave. For a man of few words, he knew how to get his message across. Whether he admitted it or not, she knew that this was his way of apologizing for his earlier bad temper. She felt suddenly much more optimistic about the future.

She set the hat on her head and tilted it at a dashing angle before tipping her head back to smile up at him.

"What do you think? Is it the real me?"

Ryder looked at her delicate features, topped by the simple straw hat. Her mouth was turned up in a wide smile, her eyes sparkled with pleasure and he felt a definite sinking sensation in his stomach. How was he supposed to keep her at a distance when everything about her drew him closer? His face softened in a smile that almost took Cally's breath away.

"It's the real you," he assured her. He glanced away, breaking the spell that was threatening to weave its way between them. "Tomás has demanded your presence at dinner again tonight." He brought the words out slowly, reluctant to puncture her mood.

Her face closed up, just as he'd known it would. He cursed mentally and reached for his cigarettes. She reached up and took off the hat, setting it on the cot and clasping her fingers together against her knees. She was staring at the floor but he didn't need to see her expression to know what she was thinking. He lit a cigarette and tossed the match into a makeshift ashtray. He inhaled deeply, wishing the acrid smoke could burn away this need to protect her, this urge to hold her and tell her that everything was going to be all right.

"Why does he want me there?" She'd managed to avoid Tomás since the day he came and demanded to know if her "father" had a heart condition.

"He's angry," Ryder admitted reluctantly. "He still hasn't been able to deliver the ransom demands. If this goes on much longer, he's going to look like a fool. He's kidnapped you but he can't even make his demands known, let alone get the money. I think he's just cracking the whip a little by demanding your presence. It will make him feel like a big man."

"You'll be there, won't you?" She looked up, not even caring if he could read the plea in her eyes.

"Sure." He didn't want to see the relief spill into her face. He didn't want her to depend on him. Or believe in him. He stubbed out his cigarette with more force than necessary. "Come on, let's get this over with."

Nothing Ryder had said had prepared Cally for the wave of hostility that hit her with Tomás's greeting. He saw her as the source of his embarrassment. He was losing face with his men and she was the cause of it.

Her eyes had barely made the adjustment from the twilight outside to the light inside the shack, when Tomás's fingers closed around her wrist. Unlike the way Ryder held her arm, there was nothing comforting about this grip.

Tomás leaned toward her, his sour breath seeming to swallow the air so that there was nothing left for her to breathe. She shrank back, unconsciously seeking the support of Ryder's presence at her back. He didn't move, didn't speak and she didn't know if that was because he was indifferent to Tomás's actions or because he didn't dare do anything about them.

Tomás's eyes bored into hers. "Your father is still ill, Señorita Wellington. They say he cannot be disturbed. My man has not been able to give him the note demanding money for your safety."

"I'm sorry." Cally didn't know if that was what he wanted her to say but it was the only thing that came to mind. His hand tightened sharply on her arm.

"You will be very sorry, señorita. Your father is a very smart man. What if he is stalling for time? That would make me very unhappy. I wonder if perhaps he would recover more quickly if I sent him his daughter's finger to show that we are very serious."

Cally swayed and Ryder's hand tightened gently on her upper arm, as if reminding her that she was not alone. "M-My father has a heart condition. He . . . he had a spell like this a year ago." She couldn't drag her eyes away from the burning hatred in Tomás's.

"Tomás, *querido,* have we been together so long that you can ignore me when I come into the room?" Elena's husky complaint broke the tension that had been building. Tomás stared at Cally a moment longer as if hoping to drag some truth out of her with the power of his gaze alone. His fingers tightened viciously on her wrist until Cally was sure she could feel the bones cracking under the strain. Just before the pain reached an unbearable level, he released her and turned away.

Cally's knees threatened to buckle and Ryder gave her unobtrusive support. She could feel the tension that hummed through his muscles but she didn't even try to guess the source. All that mattered was that he was there, that she didn't have to face Tomás completely alone.

After that beginning, she wasn't even aware of the food set in front of her. Her wrist ached with a steady throb that seemed to spread through her body until it felt as if every bone, every muscle had picked up the same pounding rhythm. She kept her head down, trying to shrink into the woodwork. With Elena present, there wasn't much chance that Tomás would bother with Cally, not even for the pleasure of relieving his anger, but she wasn't going to do anything to draw attention to herself.

After the meal, Tomás pushed his chair back from the table, belching loudly as he reached for a cigar. Ryder pulled out his cigarettes. Elena wiped a piece of bread around her plate, sopping up the last of the thin gravy and Cally stared at the table, praying for the evening to be over. All she wanted was to be safe and sound back in Ryder's tent, away from Tomás's anger.

It seemed as if the time crawled by as the two men smoked and talked about the possibility of the government mounting another concerted effort to destroy Tomás's band. They spoke Spanish and, since Cally wasn't supposed to understand the language, she was saved from any possibility of having to participate.

When, at last, Ryder stubbed his cigarette out in his plate and stood up, she had to swallow a sob of relief. She didn't say good-bye to either Elena or Tomás but nobody seemed to expect it of her. Ryder led her through the door and down the rickety steps and Cally could feel her knees weakening with every step. She stumbled and his hand tightened in warning on her arm.

"Keep walking. If you fall, I swear to God, I'll drag you the rest of the way." The harsh words had the desired effect. Though her knees didn't stop shaking, they carried her the rest of the way to the tent. Once inside, she stumbled through the darkness, collapsing on the cot while Ryder lit the lantern. The golden glow of light did nothing to dispel the darkness that had settled in her chest.

Tonight, she'd realized just how foolish it was to put her faith in Ryder. Even if he wanted to help her, there wouldn't be much that he could do if Tomás should decide that it would be expedient to kill her. He was, in a way, as helpless as she was.

"He really hates me."

"It has nothing to do with you personally." He shook out the match and dropped it in the ashtray before turning toward her. His heart twisted with pain. The golden spill of light couldn't add color to her face. Her cheeks were pallid, her eyes a dark, frightened contrast.

"It seems personal to me when he's talking about cutting off *my* finger. You can't get much more personal than that." Her voice quavered on the macabre joke and she shut her eyes, struggling for control.

"We'd better get to bed."

"It's still early." The words weren't a protest but it seemed necessary to say something. It was clear that he didn't plan on discussing Tomás with her anymore.

"I have to be up early tomorrow." The truth was that he wanted the protection of darkness. With the lantern lit, he could see her fright. It made him want to do something he'd regret, like put his arms around her and promise her he'd take care of her.

A few minutes later, he blew out the lamp and lay down on the sleeping bag. If he'd hoped that the darkness would make him less aware of her, he was doomed to disappointment. He seemed to hear every breath she took, every little shift of her body on the narrow cot. He closed his eyes, cursing the way his body stirred in response to her nearness.

"Ryder?" Her voice seemed to wash over him and he groped for his cigarettes. Maybe nicotine would block out her pull.

"Yeah?"

"It's an unusual name. Where did you get it?" Despite himself, his mouth twisted in a smile. It was obvious that she hadn't planned on what to say when she spoke his name. It reminded him of a little girl, trying to delay bedtime by asking for a story. He lit the cigarette before answering.

"It's a family name. My full name is actually John Ryder Allen but my father's name is John so my parents avoided confusion by calling me Ryder."

"John Ryder Allen. Sounds like a character out of a James Bond movie."

"Appropriate, I guess. Maybe my parents planned it that way."

"Maybe." He could almost hear her trying to think of something else to say. She seemed to want to know that she wasn't alone tonight and who could blame her? She was too young to be facing this situation. A situation that would have sent a lot of people into fits of hysteria. She'd held up with remarkable strength. He could indulge her tonight.

"What's Cally short for?"

Her soft giggle made him smile but it also tightened his fingers on the cigarette. It bothered him that she could affect him so effortlessly. Did she know that when he saw her smile he wanted to taste the curve of her mouth, that he wanted to know how her laughter felt when her body was pressed to his?

"Calliope." He had to drag his mind back to the subject at hand, ignoring the insistent throb of his body.

"Calliope? As in circus music?"

"Certainly not. As in the Greek muse of heroic poetry."

"Of course."

She giggled again at his blank tone. "Daddy was not only an archaeologist, he was also a poetry lover. Mother got pregnant while they were on a dig in Greece and, when I was born, he thought it was a good idea to name me after a muse of poetry." She stifled a yawn. "I never quite forgave Mama for not discouraging him."

"A muse of poetry. There are worse things to be named after.

Long lines of cliff breaking have left a chasm;
And in the chasm are foam and yellow sands;
Beyond, red roofs about a narrow wharf
In cluster; then a moulder'd church; and higher
A long street climbs to one tall-tower'd mill;
And high in heaven behind it a gray down
With Danish barrows; and a hazelwood,
By autumn nutters haunted, flourishes
Green in a cuplike hollow of the down."

Cally swallowed another yawn, her attention caught. Around them, the camp was quiet, nothing to distract her from the hypnotic rhythm of Ryder's voice as he recited Tennyson's "Enoch Arden." As the story spun out of the beautiful Annie and the two friends who loved her, Cally was able to forget reality and lose herself in the haunting love story.

Ryder let his voice trail off with the poem only

half told. Across the tent, Cally's breath was shallow and even. He reached out in the darkness, finding his cigarettes and lighting one. In the flare of the match, his face was all hard planes and angles, the dark slash of his mustache concealing any softness that might have been revealed by his mouth.

Tomás was losing patience. Something had to happen soon. He was running out of time. There had to be a way to do his job and get Cally out alive at the same time. He just hadn't seen it yet. But he'd find it. He had to find it.

Cally shifted in her sleep, murmuring softly. The cigarette stopped halfway to his mouth while he listened. When she settled again, he drew deeply, welcoming the harsh smoke in his throat. He was losing control of things. Events were piling up.

Events he could manipulate but it was his own feelings that worried him. It didn't pay to get involved. He couldn't afford to get involved. But he had a sinking feeling that the warning came too late.

CHAPTER SIX

Cally ran the comb through her hair, counting each stroke as if her life depended on it. Perhaps her sanity did. Ten days. Ten days and she was still alive. Perhaps she should be grateful. But it was getting more and more difficult to be grateful for anything, even life.

Ten days. It seemed like ten years. It was hard to remember that she'd ever had another life. She might have been living in this tent her whole life. Traveling between the tent and Elena's shack, playing endless games of solitaire, clinging to those times that Ryder was with her. The rest of the time seemed like a faded nightmare but he brought everything into sharp focus.

She no longer questioned her trust in him. She couldn't question it. She had to believe in him or give up all hope. She ran her thumb along the teeth of the comb, her eyes focused on nothing. He was due back soon. It was almost time for lunch. She knew when to expect him without the aid of a watch. She'd developed an inner clock that kept her in tune with the stark rhythms of existence here.

She reached up and separated her hair into three sections but her hands dropped away before she started braiding. It hardly seemed worth the effort. What difference did it make whether or not her hair was braided or her face was washed? It didn't even matter whether she ate or not. She was going to die in this horrible place. The longer she was here, the harder it was to believe anything else. Even that thought didn't stir any real emotion.

The realization that she could contemplate her own death with total equanimity was enough to snap her out of her stupor. She picked up the comb and squeezed it, deliberately letting the teeth dig into her palm. She had to stop thinking like this. She took a deep breath and forced herself to sit upright. Thinking like this wasn't going to do her any good at all.

She had to try and believe that Ryder was going to help her get out of this. She just had to believe that. Cally brushed her hair back from her face, her expression brightening when she heard footsteps outside the tent. The food he would be bringing didn't interest her but the break in the day's monotony and the promise of his company gave her a quick boost of optimism. When he was with her it wasn't so hard to believe that she'd survive.

She tugged at the collar of her shirt as the footsteps outside stopped. There wasn't much she could do about her clothing but he wouldn't be expecting any sartorial splendor. Her face was revealingly eager as she looked toward the door.

But it wasn't Ryder who stepped through the opening. Cally's smile faded.

"Who are you?"

"I have brought your lunch, señorita." He smiled, revealing yellowed teeth and an expanse of gum. He was short, with greasy hair and a grubby, unwashed look that made her skin crawl but he looked much like the other men she'd seen on her short trips through camp. Then, Ryder had always been next to her and she'd felt safe, protected by his presence.

"Where's Rico?" She stumbled over the name.

"Busy." The grin widened and she wondered if he was trying to reassure her. If so, it wasn't working. She felt distinctly uneasy but he *was* carrying the usual plate of tortillas and beans. Maybe Ryder *had* sent him.

She stood up and reached for the plate, carefully setting her fingers opposite his to avoid any possibility of contact. "Thank you."

He released the plate but his hand came up to catch a long strand of hair. "Beautiful."

Cally froze, her fingers tightening on the chipped plate. He was just trying to be friendly, she told herself. She couldn't afford to make a production out of this. "Thank you." Her smile was little more than a pained stretching of her lips. She stepped back but his fingers tightened on her hair and she was forced to stop.

"Please let go of my hair." She tried to keep her

tone calm but she could hear the strain in her voice. Panic was beginning to bubble up in her throat.

His fingers didn't move and she slowly brought her eyes up to his. He was still smiling but the look in his eyes was far from friendly. He stepped closer and, mixed with the earthy scent of beans and tortillas, she could smell the sourness of his unwashed body.

"Rico will kill you." His eyes flickered and Cally almost dared to hope. But then his mouth tightened and his chest puffed out.

"Rico is not here. There is just you and me. Besides, you are nothing. Tomás is soon to kill you anyway. Rico has no right to keep such a *bonita* prisoner all for himself."

Cally opened her mouth to scream but he read the intention in her eyes and his hand left her hair to slam down across her mouth. She tasted blood as her lips were ground back against her teeth. She dropped the plate, hearing it shatter as it hit the ground but her captor used his free hand to circle her back, crushing her to his chest, pinning her arms between them.

She struggled but there was nowhere to go. He grinned down at her, his eyes gleaming with pleasure at her helplessness and her fear.

"Your skin is so soft. Is it like that all over your body?"

Cally stopped struggling, realizing that he was enjoying her helplessness. Where was Ryder?

* * *

Ryder leaned his shoulder against the doorjamb and let his eyes move around the small room. The little building where Tomás kept weapons was the only building in the camp that could be termed solid and it was also heavily guarded. Stacked around the walls were wooden crates filled with enough arms to lay waste to a small city.

"Our friends came through for us, ay Rico?" Ryder's eyes shifted to Tomás and he nodded. Not by so much as a flicker of an eyelid did he reveal how appalled he was to think of this kind of destruction in Tomás's grubby little hands.

He stepped into the room and crossed to the boxes, ostensibly to examine the imprints identifying their contents. What he was really looking for was an indication of where Tomás was hiding his plans. He knew the little braggart kept written plans, detailing his next move against the government.

For the past two years, Tomás had been getting support from various sources dedicated to the cause of "freedom." A year ago, it had become fairly clear that he was becoming a force to be reckoned with in the political future of the country. That was when Ryder had been sent to join his ragtag band and keep an eye on what he was doing. Now, Tomás's sources had decided that the time had come for him to become more than just a major annoyance to the government. Indications were that Tomás and several other guerrilla groups were planning to band together for an attempt to overthrow the shaky government.

For a move like that, Tomás would have written plans and Ryder needed to get a look at them. So where would Tomás hide them? He leaned his hips on a box of grenades and crossed his arms over his chest, looking at Tomás.

"A lot of firepower. When will we need this?"

"Soon, Rico, soon." Tomás smiled. "I will tell you when it is time."

Ryder shrugged as if it didn't matter to him. His eyes continued to search the room, looking for a likely hiding place. But the papers were forgotten with Tomás's next words.

"How is our little guest?"

Ryder's gaze sharpened and the hair on the back of his neck lifted. He sensed danger in the simple question. He shrugged. "She's fine." He remembered the dark bruises that circled her wrist from Tomás's fingers and he swallowed a surprisingly strong surge of anger.

Tomás nodded. "My man in the capital is going to try one more time to give her father our demands."

"And then?"

Tomás shrugged. "And then I think perhaps it will be time to do something about her. She is not useful to us if we cannot get her father to pay for her. And there is much grumbling among the men. They are not happy that you do not share her with them."

Ryder's mouth curved in a slow smile. "Let

them say something to me." Tomás's eyes met his and then flickered away. There was something about this big American that made him very uneasy sometimes.

"I cannot have my men unhappy." He rocked back and forth, the floorboard creaking under him as Ryder reached for his cigarettes. It was either that or reach for the little snake's throat. His hands froze.

The scream held pure terror.

He was out the door before the last note had faded from the camp. He knew it was Cally, knew it with absolute certainty and the way his heart was pounding had nothing to do with the sprint across the camp. In the seconds it took him to race the distance to his tent, his mind presented him with half a hundred possibilities, culled from too many years of dealing with the dark side of human nature.

He was still several feet from the tent when the flap was thrust violently outward and a man sprawled out into the dirt. Cally was right behind him and Ryder skidded to a halt to avoid barreling into her. Her face was stark white, her hair a tangled mass on her shoulders. One sleeve of the shirt he'd given her was half torn and several of the buttons were gone. There was a long, angry-looking scratch that started at her collarbone and disappeared into the front of the shirt which she clutched together in a white-knuckled grip. Her eyes were wide gray pools against the pallor of her skin and a trickle of blood ran from her lower lip to her chin.

"Thank heavens I took that martial arts class last summer." She laughed and it was easy to hear the note of hysteria in the sound.

"Are you all right?" He didn't even question the urgency he felt.

"I thought it was you and then he said that you had sent him with lunch. It's on the floor. I suppose the maid will object. I was so frightened. I'm not sure what I did. I just knew I had to get him away from me."

It wasn't hard to piece together the garbled explanation and Ryder felt his rage build. That Cally was essentially uninjured didn't alleviate his anger. He turned to where the would-be rapist still lay in the dirt. The man had rolled onto his back and was in the process of sitting up, obviously dazed by the sudden reversal of roles.

Ryder's size-eleven boot caught him squarely across the chest, smashing him back down into the dirt. Ryder hadn't even been aware of drawing his knife sometime during the mad dash across camp but there it was in his hand. The haft fit his palm comfortably and the weight of it felt just right in his hand.

He crouched beside the other man, resting the point of the razor-sharp blade with gentle delicacy just against the man's jugular vein. The fallen one blinked and started to shake his head to clear his vision and then stopped as he felt the lethal pressure at his throat. His eyes widened in terror.

Ryder's expression was calm, almost serene as he looked down into the man's eyes.

"You are a very lucky man, Felipe."

Felipe did not look like he agreed but he wasn't about to argue. With the big knife at his throat, if Ryder said he was lucky, he wasn't going to disagree.

"Do you know why you are lucky?" Felipe didn't seem inclined to shake his head but Ryder didn't bother to wait for an answer. He continued in that same deadly quiet tone. "You are lucky that she took care of you herself. I would not have been so gentle."

The knife pressed a bit deeper and Felipe appeared to stop breathing. A crowd had gathered around the two men but neither of them was aware of it.

"I am sorry, Rico." Felipe barely whispered the words, all too aware of the blade at his throat.

"You are very sorry, Felipe." Ryder continued to stare into the fallen man's eyes, impressing on him just how lucky he was that Cally had defended herself. Sweat dripped off Felipe's brow, running into the greasy darkness of his hair.

"Let him go, Rico. I do not have so many men that I can afford to have them killing each other." Tomás's voice interrupted the tension building between them.

Ryder hesitated for a long moment, as if contemplating the possibility of slicing Felipe into sirloins and feeding him to the dogs. His movements were slow and reluctant as he stood up and took a step away. Felipe lay where he was for a moment as if he couldn't quite believe that he was still alive and then he rose cautiously to his feet and scuttled out of sight. A sigh rippled through the crowd, some disappointment that the excitement was over with. For a moment, the monotony of life had been eased.

Ryder slid the knife slowly back into its sheath, balancing lightly on the balls of his feet, feeling adrenaline still pounding in his veins.

"Remember that the girl is not yours to keep, Rico."

Ryder dragged his gaze away from the place where Felipe had vanished and met Tomás's eyes.

"As long as she is here, Tomás, she is mine and I will kill the next man to touch her."

He turned without waiting for Tomás's reaction and slid his arm around Cally's shoulders, prying her hand lose from its death grip on the side of the tent. He eased her into the tent, aware of the crowd dispersing behind them.

The interior of the tent was a shambles, a testament to the struggle that had gone on, and he had to swallow down a fresh wave of anger. He set his foot against the overturned cot to tilt it upright again. He sat Cally down on the edge of it, concerned by the tremors that shook her slender frame.

He scrabbled through the mess to find the tube of first-aid cream and then returned to crouch in front of her, easing her fingers away from the front of her shirt and slipping the garment off her shoulders. His jaw clenched as he looked at the scratch that ran from her collarbone down to the upper swell of her breast, stopping just above the lace of her bra.

"This must have hurt like hell."

"Yes. No. I don't remember." Her voice was tight and pitched a little too high and he knew that she was holding on to her control with sheer will-power. It wouldn't take much to shatter that control. "I'm sorry about the mess." The grave apology was offered with absolute sincerity, as if she expected him to be upset.

"Don't worry about it. This may sting." She didn't show any reaction when he gently applied the cream to the angry cut and he knew she was still in shock.

"I shouldn't have let him in. But he didn't knock and I thought he was you. I don't know what he would have knocked on." The question seemed to bother her. Ryder wished that he'd slit Felipe's throat when he'd had the chance.

"It doesn't matter." He capped the first-aid cream and set it aside before reaching for the canteen. He dampened the tail of her shirt and began dabbing at the blood on her chin. She fell silent and it wasn't until the first shining tear slid past her mouth that he realized she was crying. He lifted his gaze, feeling his heart twist with pity. Her eyes were shut and the tears seeped from beneath her lids in a slow, painful flood.

"Oh hell."

"I'm sorry." Her lashes flickered upward and he could see the despair in her eyes. "I'm sorry."

"Stop saying you're sorry!" He dropped her shirttail but continued to crouch in front of her. His hands hung awkwardly in midair for a moment before he forced them down to rest on his knees.

"I just wish he'd kill me. I'm so tired of being scared. He's going to do it sooner or later so why doesn't he do it now?" Her breath caught in a sob and the tears continued to wash down her face in a silvery tide.

Ryder lifted his hands hesitantly, uncertain of what he planned to do with them. Cally leaned toward him and, a moment later, her face was buried in his shoulder without him being quite sure of how the move had been made. He shifted until he was sitting next to her on the cot, his arms around her slender body. She cried without fanfare, soft sobs that seemed so hopeless that they tore at his heart.

It seemed very intimate somehow. Her tears on his skin. His hand was clumsy as he brushed the hair back from her face, feeling it cling to his fingers like a gossamer ribbon tying them together. He let her cry out all the tension and fears she'd been holding inside, only now realizing how much her control had been costing her.

"It's going to be all right. I won't let anything happen to you." The words had scarcely left his mouth before he was wondering if he'd be able to keep the promise. But he knew he would do any-

118

thing he had to to make sure that she was protected.

His hand cupped the back of her head, tilting her face up to his. He waited until she opened her eyes to look at him before reiterating the promise. "I won't let anything happen to you. We're going to get you out of here."

The look she gave him was so full of emotion—trust, lingering fear, need—that he felt all his control slipping away. His head lowered and Cally's eyes fluttered shut again. His mustache brushed across her eyelids as he dried the last of her tears with his mouth.

Her skin was incredibly soft beneath his lips. He slid his hands deeper into the satin fall of her hair, sifting it through his fingers like fine silk. His mouth trailed down her cheek to hover over her mouth. If he kissed her, he knew he would have lost the silent battle he'd been fighting since the first moment he'd seen her.

His mouth dipped slowly, inevitably toward hers. At the first touch of his mouth, Cally seemed to melt toward him. Her hands slid up his shirt-front to circle his neck, her fingers burrowing into the thick black hair at the base of his skull. Ryder fought for control. He shouldn't be doing this. Things were complicated enough. But the protests seemed far off and weak compared to the softness of her mouth beneath his.

The adrenaline that had surged through him outside rushed into his veins and it took all his ragged self-control to keep from crushing her mouth beneath his. He'd wanted her for so long. The sweet taste of her mouth made him want more. He wanted her beneath him, her body open to his. He wanted to feel her hair spread like a silk cape across his chest.

The interior of the tent was dim, despite the sunshine outside. Hot and dim, creating a warm cocoon that made it easy to forget the rest of the world. And, for just a little while, that was what he let himself do. He forgot all the reasons why this was wrong, all the arguments, and just savored the feel of her against him.

His tongue ran along the inside of her lip, gently exploring the shallow cut left by Felipe's hand. How dare another man touch her? Cally's mouth opened to him and the kiss deepened slowly. It seemed inevitable that she should fit his arms so perfectly. Inevitable that her mouth should taste sweeter than any other. Her body nestled so comfortably against his, so perfectly. He had only to slide the loose shirt away and his hands would be free to explore every gentle curve. How could he have waited so long for this? She was his. Only his.

The thought was so positive that it snapped him out of the spell that was weaving itself around them. He couldn't afford to think like that. They had been thrown together but the reality was that they were worlds apart. He'd seen and done too much in his lifetime.

She sighed a protest as his mouth left hers, his hands easing away from the tempting web of her hair. Her lashes fluttered and then lifted and Ryder was almost lost in the smoky invitation of her eyes. It took every ounce of his willpower to back away until they were no longer touching. His eyes held hers for a long moment, a part of him savoring her obvious reluctance to let him go. He turned away before he could give in to temptation.

He reached for his duffel bag, slipping his hand into a deep side pocket and coming up with a small bottle of amber-colored liquid. Another brief search and he found a small metal cup. He splashed some of the liquid into the cup and handed it to Cally.

"A medicinal dose of brandy is always good for the nerves."

She took the cup without comment, though it occurred to her that his kiss had probably done more for her nerves than an entire bottle of brandy could have accomplished. The nightmare with Felipe was already beginning to fade. She took a sip of the brandy, choking slightly as the alcohol evaporated in her throat.

Ryder grinned at her watering eyes. "See, good for the nerves."

"With enough of this, I won't even be able to tell that I *have* nerves." Her eyes lingered on his smile, savoring the rare softness of his mouth. It was frightening to realize that she was beginning to store up his smiles as if they were a treasure she was hoarding.

Ryder stayed with her the rest of the afternoon and, though there was a lingering tension about him, he went out of his way to entertain her, perhaps trying to prevent her from dwelling on what had almost happened to her.

Cally was honest with herself and admitted that she didn't care what his reasons were. All that mattered was that she wasn't left alone. She helped him straighten up the mess left by her struggle with Felipe, trying not to remember what had happened.

She was both surprised and grateful when he suggested that they play a game of cards. She'd expected him to leave and she'd promised herself that she wouldn't ask him to stay but she was glad she didn't have to put her determination to the test.

"You cheated!" She threw down her cards and glared at him.

"What makes you say that?" His expression was bland as he gathered the cards together and began to shuffle.

"Because the odds against getting two royal flushes in a row are astronomical."

"Maybe I'm just very lucky."

"And maybe you cheated."

His grin showed not a trace of remorse. "This *is* cutthroat poker, isn't it?"

"You're a cardsharp."

"I'm just lucky." He splayed the cards out and then gathered them up with a flourish, shuffling them so rapidly Cally was sure she could see the spots flying off them. She would never have guessed that his square hands, which held a knife so comfortably, could handle a deck of cards with equal ease. For a few minutes, he played with the cards, making them do everything but sit up and sing.

"Where did you learn to do that?"

He manipulated the cards and then spread them out in front of her, neatly arranged by suit. "I spent some time as a dealer in Monte Carlo."

She pulled her eyes from the cards and looked at him, trying to imagine him in a tuxedo. Yes, she could see him standing behind a black-jack table, his hair cut shorter and his mustache neatly trimmed. He'd look as comfortable there as he did here in his worn khakis.

"They taught you to cheat at cards in Monte Carlo?"

"Not exactly. But you have to know the cards very well to be able to spot things that aren't quite right. Besides, these cards are marked."

The announcement was so casual that it took Cally a moment to register what he'd said. She stared at the deck for a moment and then looked up at him, meeting the bland look in his eyes.

"You *have* been cheating!"

"The odds against getting two royal flushes in a row are astronomical," he quoted. He ducked the pillow she flung at his head.

If his intention was to distract her and help her forget, he succeeded. By the time he blew out the lantern, plunging the tent into darkness, Cally was able to close her eyes without panicking. As she drifted off to sleep, the last thing she thought of was the enticing feel of Ryder's mustache against her skin.

CHAPTER SEVEN

Ryder flattened himself against the side of the shack, willing himself to blend into the shadows there as the guard paused only a few feet from him to light a cigarette. The light of the full tropical moon was bright and Ryder could only pray that the shadow was deep enough to hide him. The guards all had orders to shoot first and ask questions later. His hand crept down his side to where his knife was sheathed. A knife had the advantage of being a silent killer, but he'd have to be absolutely sure of his aim.

The guard muttered a curse as his match blew out before he could get the cigarette lit. He struck another match and this time succeeded. Ryder's nose twitched as a breeze blew the smoke his direction, wafting it past his face as if pointing a ghostly finger to his hiding place. The guard shook the match and tossed it casually over his shoulder. It landed within an inch of Ryder's boot. His eyes dropped and he saw that the flame had not gone out. It lay like a tiny beacon. If the guard should see it . . . His mouth tasted coppery as he shifted his foot the smallest amount and crushed the flickering light.

After what seemed like hours, the guard turned and continued his stroll around the shack. Ryder had timed it and he knew exactly how long he'd have to get the door of the little building open and slip inside before the man circled back around. It wasn't long enough but it would have to do.

He worked quickly but methodically, forcing himself not to hurry too much as he worked the lockpick in the heavy padlock. Sweat trickled down his cheek, streaking the soot he'd applied to darken his face. Just a few more seconds. He could hear the guard returning, his footsteps unnaturally loud in the night quiet camp.

The padlock sprang apart and he slipped into the hut, easing the door shut as the guard stepped around the corner of the building. Ryder stood in the darkness, hardly daring to breathe. What if the man noticed that the padlock wasn't closed? Minutes ticked by. His fingers closed around the haft of the knife. If the guard came up to the door to examine the lock, he might be able to jerk him into the room and dispose of him before he could make some noise that would alert the camp.

The footsteps resumed, circling around the building. Ryder cracked the door just enough to grab the lock and twist it together so that it gave the appearance of being shut. He reached into his back pocket and took out a penlight, flicking on the narrow beam. There were no windows in the room but he didn't want to take a chance on the light being seen through some crack in the walls so he shielded the bulb with his hands, reducing the light to a mere glow.

This wasn't the way he'd have chosen to work things. He'd planned on getting Tomás to confide in him. It would have been much safer that way. But there wasn't time for that. The events of the day had made that more than clear. Tomás could decide at any moment that Cally was no longer useful and then the only thing he would be able to do would be to get himself killed trying to protect her. Which is just what he'd do, he admitted ruefully.

Earlier he'd lain on the sleeping bag listening to Cally's quiet breathing and trying to decide just how to handle this suddenly explosive situation. There was Tomás to worry about but he also knew that Cally had reached the end of her rope. If he didn't get her out now, she was going to break down completely. And it surprised him to discover that her mental state carried a lot of weight in his calculations. So much for all those years of training that taught him that the job came first, before all other considerations.

There had to be a way to protect Cally and still do his job. If only he knew where Tomás kept his plans. He reached for a cigarette and then stopped. As sharp as if standing in front of him, he saw Tomás in the hut. Rocking back on his heels, the floorboard creaking beneath him. He'd smiled so smugly when he said that he would reveal his plans when the time was right. Had he looked at his feet then? Ryder closed his eyes, the cigarette forgotten. He was almost certain that Tomás had looked down. The paper could be under the floorboard. It would have amused Tomás to know that the papers were right under his feet as they were talking.

Did he dare take a chance on breaking into the hut? Cally shifted and moaned in her sleep and the question was answered for him. He had to get her out of here. He sat up, careful to make no noise as he reached for his boots. He debated for a moment about waking Cally and then decided not to. It could take quite some time for what he had in mind. Let her sleep. He shifted through his duffel bag, finding the things he needed by feel. It took only seconds to blacken his face with soot and then he was slipping out of the tent, keeping to the shadows . . .

Now, he directed the light around the floor, trying to remember exactly where Tomás had been standing. There. That was the floorboard. He dropped to his knees and ran his fingertips along the edge of the board. His teeth flashed in a grin as he felt the shallow depression that gave him room to get his fingers beneath the board. The board came up without a sound and he picked up the penlight and flashed it into the compartment he'd exposed.

His mouth puckered in a silent whistle. Tomás had gotten more than weapons from his "friends." He picked up a stack of bills and riffled through it. There was a lot of currency here. He dropped the money back into the stack and reached for the sheaf of papers. Flipping it open, he allowed himself a grin. This was what he was after. He reached into his pocket and pulled out a slim camera, hardly the size of a cigarette pack.

He went through the papers one by one, clicking a picture of each page, trying not to think about the time that was passing. What if the guard should decide to check the door? What if someone had seen him leave the tent and had gone in to catch Cally alone and defenseless? He couldn't think of anything but the job at hand. He snapped the last picture and closed the folder, setting it back in the compartment exactly as he'd found it before easing the floorboard back into place. A simple hiding place but effective.

His knees protested when he stood up and he grimaced at the twinge of pain. Maybe he was getting too old for this job. He flashed the penlight around quickly, making sure that there were no traces of his visit and then snapped the light off and made his way back to the door.

He leaned against the door and listened, making himself be patient as he waited for the sound of the guard's footsteps. As soon as the man had gone past the front of the building, he would slip out, replace the lock and get back to his tent. There were still three or four hours of darkness left and he wanted to take advantage of every one of them.

Cally came awake suddenly, panic rushing through her veins. She couldn't breathe. Her eyes flew open on darkness and her fingers came up to claw at the hand that was planted across her mouth.

"It's all right. It's me, Ryder." It took a moment for the words to penetrate the sleep haze that fogged her mind. He loomed over her, a black shadow in the darkness of the tent. She relaxed slowly, letting her hands fall away. He waited for a moment, assuring himself that she was awake and then took his palm from her mouth.

"What is it?" She pitched her voice to a whisper, responding to the darkness and his air of secrecy.

"Get up and get dressed but don't make any noise."

He turned away and she swung her legs off the cot, obeying automatically. "What's going on?"

"We're getting out of here."

Her hands froze on the snap of her jeans. Had he said what she thought? Had he said that they were leaving? She couldn't even begin to sort out all the emotions that raced through at that thought. Relief. Fear. Confusion.

"Hurry up." His voice was an impatient rasp and Cally forced herself to swallow her questions. She dressed quickly, trying not to think about what might lie outside the safe haven of the tent.

She stood up as Ryder turned. Her eyes had adjusted to the darkness and she could see the glitter of his gaze as it skimmed over her.

"Damn. That hair stands out like a spotlight." Before she could do more than lift her hands, he'd stepped closer, scooping her hair up in his fingers and bundled it on top of her head. He picked up his hat and shoved it onto her head, stuffing loose strands of hair up beneath the crown. Cally's eyes watered but she didn't protest. He stepped back and looked at her again. She tried to look as if she were ready for anything but he shook his head again.

"Your skin isn't much better." She shut her eyes as he ran his fingers around the inside of the lamp and rubbed the results on her face. She wondered if there'd ever been any research done on the pros and cons of using lampblack as a beauty aid. This time when he stepped back to look at her, he nodded.

"You'll do." He bent to scoop up a small bundle.

"We're going to take a back route out of camp. Follow right behind me and don't say anything. I don't care if you step on an anaconda, you don't make a sound, understand?"

She nodded, her eyes wide. He hesitated for a moment, seeming to struggle with himself, and then his head dipped and he planted a firm kiss on her mouth.

"We'll get out of here." He turned and slipped out of the tent and Cally followed him without looking back. There was nothing in the tent that she wanted to remember.

She'd never realized how bright the moon could seem when you were trying not to be seen. Ryder slipped through the shadows with an ease that seemed at odds with his size. In contrast, Cally felt as if she blundered along in his wake, telegraphing their presence with every step she took.

They stopped in the shadow of a ramshackle building and Ryder's hand closed around her arm, drawing her deeper into the shadow. The tension in his fingers alerted her and she cocked her head, listening. A second later she heard footsteps. She froze, hardly daring to breathe. Were they about to be discovered? Ryder was pressing the bundle he'd taken from the tent into her hand and her fingers closed around it automatically. He didn't have to caution her to silence as the guard moved into sight.

He stopped only a few feet from them and Cally waited for him to shout his discovery of their presence. Moonlight gleamed off the barrel of the rifle slung over his shoulder. After a moment, she realized that he was turned the other way, staring at the barricade of brush that surrounded the camp. She leaned closer into the wall of the building, her nails digging into the warped wood. Beside her, Ryder was absolutely still. He might have been a statue. Sliding her gaze toward him, she couldn't detect any sign of life except the faint glitter of his eyes.

She closed her own eyes, sure that if she looked at the guard one more minute, the tension would get to her and she'd run screaming from their shallow concealment. She tried to retrace their route through the camp, trying to figure out where they were, but in the moonlight everything looked different.

The guard shifted and she held her breath. Was he pointing the rifle at them? Had they been discovered? She waited for him to shout or for the impact of a bullet but nothing happened and after a moment she dared to breathe again.

Her fingers tightened on the wall and her eyes flew open. Elena's. The wall they were leaning against was the house that Elena and Tomás shared. Ryder had said that they were taking a back way out of the camp and it made sense that it would be near Tomás's house. An escape route perhaps.

There was a stir of movement beside her and Ryder was gone. Her hand came out as if to stop him but she halted the movement. Her fingers tightened into a fist and fell to her side.

He was hardly more than a shadow himself as he left the shelter of the building. If Cally hadn't been watching him, she would never have known that he was there. The guard did not have her advantage. The man seemed to sense something at the last second but he didn't have time to turn. Ryder's hand rose and fell and there was a sickening thunk and then he was lowering the guard to the dirt.

He waved her forward and Cally forced her trembling knees to function. Seconds later, they were on the other side of the brush barrier, with only a few scratches to show where they had wiggled through the wall. Cally took a deep breath. Was it her imagination or did the air seem less confined?

Ryder searched through the bundle he'd brought from the tent, his movements quick, and Cally knew that it wasn't time to celebrate yet. She could barely see his hand as he lifted it to his mouth, cautioning her to stay silent and then gestured toward the jungle behind them. She nodded, indicating that she understood. He turned and took two steps and completely vanished!

Cally froze, staring into the blackness where he'd gone. He couldn't be far but he'd disappeared as thoroughly as if he'd never existed. She took a deep breath, fighting back the urge to blunder forward. Ryder would realize that she wasn't with him, and he'd come back for her. If she entered the jungle without knowing where she was going, she would simply get lost.

It seemed as if hours passed but it could only have been a few seconds before he appeared beside her as silently as he'd vanished. Impatience radiated from him and she didn't need light to read the question in his expression. She raised her hand to her eyes and shrugged, hoping he'd understand the problem. He nodded and reached out to grasp her hand as he stepped back into the jungle, this time taking her with him.

It might have been bright moonlight in the clearing but, beneath the forest canopy, it was dark. Not just night dark but a heavy blackness that seemed to have a substance all its own. Cally had been in jungles before but, by nightfall, she'd always been safely tucked away in a tent, with her father somewhere nearby and the other members of the dig not far away. This was the first time she'd ever been actually out in the jungle at night.

The blackness was beyond description. She had the feeling that if she reached out, she could grasp the thickness of it and draw it aside to reveal light. If it hadn't been for Ryder's hand pulling her forward, she would have been completely lost within seconds.

Ryder stopped so suddenly that she bumped into him but he seemed to be oblivious to her presence. He released her hand and she instinctively grabbed hold of his belt, not wanting to be left alone. Light flickered, just a tiny point of brightness, but it seemed dazzling after the blackness that had gone before. She could see Ryder's hands in the light but not much else. He was consulting a compass. The light flicked out and he started forward again, reaching out to grasp her wrist.

The pattern continued. They walked for a distance and he would stop and consult the compass and then they walked some more. Cally waited until the third time he stopped, sure that they were far enough from the camp to dare a whisper. The light flicked on in his hands and he studied the compass.

"How can you see where we're going? It's pitch black."

The light flicked upward, giving her a glimpse of his face, eyes shielded by lightweight glasses. "Infrared lenses."

He flashed the light around, creating monstrous shapes out of the jungle growth. He gave a pleased murmur and strode to the foot of a jungle giant. Cally wrinkled her nose at the smell of rotting vegetation as he began to scoop aside the debris. He used the point of his knife to hack at the dirt and then shoveled the dirt out of the way.

He'd laid the penlight on the ground and in the diffused illumination Cally saw him pull a light-weight pack out of the hole he'd dug. He dusted off the khaki surface and quickly checked the seals before setting it aside. Moments later, the dirt had been pushed back into the hole and the leaves and vines pushed back over that.

He stood up, slinging the pack onto his back. He'd tied the bundle from the tent to his belt and he left that where it was. He consulted the compass once again and then clicked off the penlight, plunging them into darkness. His fingers closed around Cally's wrist but she hung back.

"Where did that pack come from? And where are we going?"

His hand tightened on her wrist and he tugged her forward. "Not now. You can ask questions later."

Cally swallowed her curiosity. He was right. They needed to put distance between themselves and Tomás now. It was just that she hated being in the dark, both literally and figuratively.

The pace he set was rapid and it was a constant effort for her to avoid stumbling over the roots and vines that littered the forest floor. She'd spent ten days confined in an area where there wasn't even room to pace and her legs soon protested this sudden exercise. She said nothing, only gritted her teeth and forced herself to keep up the pace he set.

By the time he stopped, she was dazed with exhaustion. She'd long since stopped thinking of anything except the necessity of putting one foot in front of another. The lightweight boots that had seemed so perfect for a trip to look at her father's old site felt like dead weight dragging her feet down. She was so absorbed in the simple act of walking that she was oblivious to the slow graying of the blackness around them.

"We'll stop here for a few hours." The words didn't penetrate in time to prevent her from running into him when he stopped abruptly. He absorbed the collision, setting her back on her feet without complaint. Cally looked at "here," seeing nothing but an enormous tree whose roots spread out in huge, buttressing wings. Ryder knelt to open the pack he'd dug up while Cally tilted her head back, trying to see the top of the tree. A hundred feet above her the forest canopy cut off any further view. The branches were so festooned with plant life that it looked as if they might come crashing down under the weight they supported. Cally yawned, too tired to care.

It was only when she looked back down at Ryder that she realized that she could see again. The light was a peculiar gray green, filtered through the jungle. The sun was creeping downward through the foliage, slowly illuminating the tangle of vines and trees.

Ryder spread a thin, shiny blanket among the

huge roots, covering the ground and, hopefully, giving some protection from the abundant insect life. Once settled on the blanket, she realized that the roots formed shielding walls, so that they would only be visible to someone coming from directly in front.

"Cozy." Now that she was off her feet, she felt some of her energy returning. She was out of the guerrilla camp and nothing could dim the pleasure of that thought.

Ryder glanced around their hideaway and grunted. "It'll do." He untied the bundle from his belt and began to empty it. He handed her a thin towel that held a stack of the ubiquitous tortillas and then came up with a container of dried beef. Cally wrapped a stick of the beef in a tortilla and handed it to him. He took the makeshift sandwich without comment and continued to go through the pack.

Cally munched her cold breakfast—or was it dinner?—and watched him. It was rather like watching a magician pull tricks out of a hat. Just when she was sure there couldn't possibly be anything more in the pack, he pulled something else out.

He swallowed the last bite of tortilla and surveyed the items spread out on the blanket. Survival packs of food, a larger flashlight, a thin sleeping bag, ammunition and two guns. To this he added the things he'd brought from camp. The ammunition from his duffel bag, the dried beef, the remaining tortillas, the canteens, and the blanket from the cot. He picked up the smaller gun and weighed it in his hand before looking at her.

"Do you know how to use one of these?"

"My father taught me to shoot when I was twelve. He thought it was essential considering how much time we spent miles from civilization."

He hesitated, studying her as if his decision were based on what he saw more than what she said. After a moment, he handed her the gun and a small box of ammunition.

"Load it and keep it close. Chances are you won't need it."

Cally loaded the gun, aware of the faith he was showing in her by giving her the weapon.

"Do you think Tomás will follow us?"

"He'll follow us."

She glanced over her shoulder, half expecting to see Tomás coming at them. "Shouldn't we keep moving?"

"We've got a long way to go. I spent some time laying down a false trail and I knocked out the guards at four different places. With any luck, they won't know where we left the camp. It's not all that easy to track someone in the jungle, Tarzan movies aside."

"But won't he want to get me back? I mean, he hasn't gotten any money from Uncle Richard yet."

Ryder began loading things back into the pack. "He was getting tired of waiting." He let the comment sink in, seeing the way her features tightened as she realized what he meant. "I'm hoping that he'll decide to cut his losses. If he thinks that I fell for you and took you and ran rather than see you killed, he may decide it's not worth his time to pursue us too far."

"What else could he think?"

He hesitated before answering. "I have some information that Tomás would not want getting out."

"Information? You mean something for the people you really work for?"

"Something for the people I really work for," he acknowledged, admitting for the first time that he did work for someone else. "Try and get some sleep." He cut off the questions he could see bubbling to be asked. "I'll wake you in a couple of hours and you can keep watch while I catch a nap and then we'll go on."

"Where are we going?"

"A village. Now get some sleep."

Cally reluctantly lay down, using a rolled-up blanket for a pillow. She was asleep almost as soon as her eyes closed and Ryder allowed himself the indulgence of watching her for a moment.

She'd taken the hat off when they stopped and her hair spilled out across the dark blanket like a vein of white gold. Her face was still smudged with soot, her lashes forming dark crescents against her cheeks. She looked like a dirty angel. The unaccustomed whimsicality of the thought startled him and he dragged his eyes away from her, forcing himself to consider only those things necessary to their survival.

Had their disappearance been discovered yet? So

much depended on how much of a lead they got. His gaze returned to Cally as if drawn by a magnet. He'd gotten her and the film out of the camp. With any luck, he'd be able to get her to safety and accomplish his job at the same time.

It all depended on his survival skills and a lot of luck.

CHAPTER EIGHT

Green on green on more green. Cally had never realized that there were so many different shades of green. And it took very little time for her to wish that she never had to look at the color again. There were greens so dark they were almost black and greens so bright they almost hurt the eyes.

And the quiet. Where was all the noise in Tarzan's jungles? It was eerily silent. They might have been moving through a film set waiting for Johnny Weissmuller to swing in on a vine and start the action. The occasional scream of some unseen bird only served to emphasize the silence that followed.

Cally would almost have welcomed the roar of a lion or a tiger's cough—never mind that neither was likely to show up in Central America. Almost anything to break the quiet. Ahead of her, Ryder kept a slow but steady pace. The heavy canopy of leaves and vines cast a shade so thick that the growth on the ground was minimal. Walking was not a big problem, if you discounted the fact that the humidity sometimes rose to at least five hundred percent. The dampness was ever-present and draining.

Two hours' sleep had not been enough to make up for the tension of their escape. That was all the time Ryder had allowed before waking her. He'd told her to wake him in two hours but he'd barely slept an hour before shaking himself awake. Cally envied his alert appearance. She felt like a slice of week-old bread, tired and slightly moldy around the edges.

It was impossible to tell what time it was. The sunlight that filtered through to the forest floor didn't seem to change from morning to afternoon. It appeared and you knew it was morning and, when it disappeared, you knew it was night. They had eaten another tortilla and some of the dried beef before leaving their resting place at the base of the giant tree, but Cally's stomach was beginning to hint that perhaps it was time to eat again. Looking ahead at Ryder's solid back, she wondered if she dared to suggest that they might pause long enough to get some food out of his pack.

He stopped and she thought he must have read her mind. She opened her mouth to make some facetious comment about finding a restaurant but something in the waiting quality of his stillness stopped the words before she could even decide exactly what she'd planned to say.

He took a quick backward step, his hand dipping to his waistband and coming up with the gun that had been tucked there. Another backward step and he reached out to grab her arm, pulling her with him as they stepped off the path he'd been following and into the shadows of a huge palm.

Cally opened her mouth to whisper a question but all that came out was a muffled gasp as he suddenly spun her around, shoving her to the ground and crushing her into the leaves and vines with his weight as he lay over her.

Seconds later, she heard the crunch of boots and whispered voices and realized what was happening. Tomás had come looking for them, just as Ryder had promised. It had to be his men whose boots sounded so close. Ryder's body tightened over hers, one arm thrown above her head, his other hand clutching the pistol against her side. She realized what he was doing and prayed that it worked. His fatigues would blend in with the jungle floor far better than her jeans and shirt. He was literally hiding her with his body.

She shut her eyes, praying that his stratagem worked. The footsteps came to a halt and Cally quit breathing. There was a murmur of voices but the rushing in her ears was too loud for her to hear what was being said. Seconds ticked by, each one bringing them closer to discovery. Abruptly, the men moved off.

Cally opened her eyes as Ryder's weight lifted. Whatever thoughts had been in her head, they disappeared when she met the midnight of his gaze. Had anyone ever had eyes of that particular shade? She opened her mouth, unsure what she planned to say but wanting to break the tension. His eyes darkened in warning and then his mouth came down on hers, cutting off her voice.

If his intention had been to silence her, he was successful. If his intention had been to make her forget the danger, he succeeded in that. And if his intention had been to send her blood racing through her veins, he did that, too.

Cally forgot that she was lying on the jungle floor, probably getting bugs of unknown lineage in her hair. She forgot the vines jabbing her in the back, the fact that their enemies were nearby. She forgot everything but the weight of his body on hers and the taste of his mouth.

She felt his shudder as the impact of the kiss went through him. His mouth hardened, his tongue flicking out to tease hers. His body seemed to grow heavier, crushing her with his strength. Her hands were caught between them and she murmured with frustration. She wanted to put her arms around him, wanted to draw him even closer.

Ryder groaned, the sound rumbling in his chest, barely audible. He dragged his mouth away and Cally was pleased to see that his breathing was almost as ragged as hers. Their eyes met and she read the disturbance in the turbulent blue of his. She could only guess at what he might read in hers.

Without a word, he lifted his weight, crouching over her for a moment, scanning the jungle around them. He stood up slowly, putting his hand down to take hers and haul her to her feet. Cally stood next to him, wondering if she'd imagined those seconds with his mouth on hers.

He put his finger to his mouth, his eyes cautioning her. Still holding her hand, he eased them around the trunk of the palm, away from the path they'd been on. They crept from tree to tree. Twice they froze, hardly daring to breathe, while boots tromped past only a few feet away.

She should have been terrified. She *was* terrified. But, somehow, with Ryder's hand on her wrist, his fingers against her pulse, it was hard to believe that they wouldn't escape. Her earlier hunger was forgotten. There were more important things to think about now.

She was beginning to think that they'd made it past the men looking for them. It had been a long time since Ryder had flattened her against a tree, his weight guarding her, holding her still. They could hear nothing except the stillness of the jungle around them. Surely they were in the clear now.

She stumbled over a vine, ducking her head to watch her feet. The adrenaline of being hunted was wearing off and weariness was taking its place. It was impossible to judge but surely it must be getting close to dark. They'd have to stop for the night.

Head down, she didn't notice Ryder stopping until his hand tightened bruisingly on her wrist. She jerked her head up, her protest dying unvoiced. A man stood not more than four feet in front of them. The first thing she noticed was the gun. It was amazing how large a rifle barrel could seem when you were looking down the business end of it. Her eyes trailed the length of it to his face, taking in the intent features, the dark eyes.

"Do not move, Rico."

Cally could only stare, wide-eyed and dazed. They'd been so close. A few feet one way or another and they might have walked past without him seeing them. The undergrowth was thick enough to conceal them. Just a few feet.

"José." Ryder's voice revealed none of the tension she felt in his fingers before he dropped her wrist. The rifle barrel jerked warningly.

"Keep your hands away from your body. Take your gun out very slowly and drop it on the ground."

"I can hardly keep my hands away and take out my gun at the same time, amigo. You should make up your mind."

The eyes behind the gun did not lighten with humor. "Do not try to be funny, Rico. Take out the gun. I do not wish to shoot you or the pretty little gringa."

Cally didn't want him to shoot her either but she didn't really like seeing Ryder ease the pistol from the holster and drop it to the ground. A sharp gesture from José and his knife followed the gun. Cally thought of the gun tucked into the back of her waistband. It had been an annoying yet comforting presence all day. Obviously José did not know of its existence. Her fingers balled into a fist but there was no way she could get her hand under her shirt to lift the weapon from its hiding place without him noticing. Why hadn't she put it somewhere more accessible?

Ryder's hands lifted and José jerked the rifle warningly. Cally could almost see his finger tightening on the trigger. In the humidity of the jungle, it was impossible not to sweat but when she felt a rivulet of moisture trickle down her face, she knew it had nothing to do with the ever-present heat.

"Just a cigarette, amigo. You don't mind if I smoke while we wait for your compadres, do you?"

José hesitated a long moment and then nodded jerkily and Ryder's hands went to his shirt pocket, carefully pulling out his cigarettes and a book of matches.

"You should not have run, Rico. Tomás is very angry."

Ryder lit the cigarette and took a deep draw, squinting against the resulting smoke. He dropped the match and then took a step forward to retrieve it from the forest floor.

"Hate to start a jungle fire." He tested the warmth of it on his fingertip and then dropped it in his pocket. He was now practically nose to nose with the rifle barrel.

"Tomás is angry, huh?"

"*Muy* angry. He wants you alive so that he may have the pleasure of watching you die."

"And you, José? Do you also wish to watch me die?"

José shrugged. "It's not what I wish. If it were

148

not for you, my little Carmelita would not be alive. But Tomás is our leader and I cannot go against him."

Ryder nodded. "I understand."

"Why did you do it, Rico? You were so devoted to the cause."

Ryder shrugged, taking another drag from the cigarette. "A woman, José."

José's eyes flickered to Cally. "She is *muy bonita,* Rico, but is she worth dying for?"

"Always, José." He put such fervor in his voice that Cally almost believed him herself. "I would ask a favor. For myself, I can face what lies ahead but do not let her go to Tomás. You must kill her yourself."

Cally couldn't believe what she was hearing. José's eyes shifted and darkened. "I do not know, Rico. Tomás wants her alive."

"Take my gun and shoot her. You can tell them that I killed her myself rather than let Tomás get hold of her."

"You must love this woman very much, Rico."

"More than life itself." His voice deepened on the words, controlled passion making his tones husky.

José's eyes moved from Cally to Ryder to the gun that lay between them. The rifle barrel wavered and she could almost see the conflict in his mind. The barrel wavered again, lowering slightly and Ryder moved so quickly, he was almost a blur. His hand jerked, flicking the burning cigarette toward José's face. The man jerked back, a startled cry escaping him. Ryder followed through the movement of the cigarette, his palm connecting with the stock of the rifle, literally slapping it out of José's hands.

Cally dove for the gun, but it wasn't needed. Both Ryder's feet left the ground, his right leg coming out, the foot catching José in the chest, knocking the other man backward into a tangle of vines and undergrowth. Before he had a chance to gather his feet under him, Ryder had him by the front of the shirt.

"I'm sorry, José." His fist connected to José's chin with a sickening crunch and José went limp. Ryder eased the other man onto the ground. He wiped the sweat from his brow and turned to find Cally with the rifle in her hands, obviously prepared to use it if necessary. His eyes darkened and he stalked across the few feet that separated them and snatched the gun from her.

"If I'd wanted your help, I'd have asked for it," he snapped.

She blinked. "I just thought . . ."

"I don't care what you thought. If I don't ask for help, don't give it to me." He thrust his fingers through his hair. "I can't believe I'm in the middle of the jungle with half an army after me and you to take care of. Why aren't you home worrying about a date or something?"

He bent to pick up his pistol and knife, carefully wiping both off before returning them to holster and sheath.

"Is he dead?"

"No, he's not dead. He'll wake up in an hour or two with a hell of a headache and make his way back to camp. And Tomás will probably kill him." He slid the strap of the rifle over his shoulder. "Let's get out of here."

Cally hesitated, looking at the fallen man. "Shouldn't we do something for him?"

"Like what? José is one of the unfortunate few who truly believe that Tomás has a great 'cause.' He'd never go with us willingly." His eyes were dark with angry regret as he looked at the other man. "He'll just have to take his chances with Tomás."

If the pace he'd set had been hard before, it was grueling now. He kept hold of her wrist, not pausing even when she stumbled. The very force of his pull helped to keep her on her feet. Cally wanted to protest. She *would* have protested, if only she'd had the breath to do so. But she knew why he was setting the pace he was. They knew that Tomás's men were right behind them.

When the filtered light began to fade, he slowed the pace slightly, finally stopping just before absolute darkness descended. He set up their tiny camp between the outstretched roots of another forest giant. The rain had held off today so the ground was relatively dry. Cally collapsed on the thin blanket, thinking that nothing had ever felt so good. Silently, Ryder handed her the canteen and usual tortillas and dried beef and she took it, trying not to think about grilled steaks and baked potatoes slathered in butter.

She could hear him moving about, shuffling things in the pack. Though he was hardly more than three feet away, the darkness was so complete that she could make out little more than his outline.

"You'd better go ahead and get some sleep now. I want to start as soon as it's light." Cally's hands closed over the sleeping bag but she hesitated before spreading it out.

"What about you?"

"I'll be fine."

"You're not going to sit up all night keeping watch, are you?"

"No, I'm not. They're not going to be hunting us in the dark."

She spread out the sleeping bag and then hesitated again. "This is the only sleeping bag. How are you going to sleep?"

"I've slept under worse conditions." There was an edge to his voice that warned her to drop it but she didn't feel right about taking his sleeping bag and leaving him with nothing. The ground might feel wonderful now but it was going to get pretty hard to sleep on.

"Maybe we could share the sleeping bag. I could take it for half the night and then . . ."

"Just shut up and lie down!" Cally jumped as his voice lashed out of the darkness. "I don't want the damn sleeping bag."

She blinked back tears, refusing to sniff. Her hands were shaking as she spread the thin pad over the ground and slid inside. It felt cozy and protected. She looked in Ryder's direction but she could see nothing to indicate his presence. She closed her eyes and was asleep before she could try to analyze his mood.

Ryder listened to her steady breathing and forced his fists to unclench, stretching out each finger individually. He leaned his head back against the thick root and closed his eyes. Sweat trickled down his forehead, though the temperature no longer warranted it. He could hear the ragged edge to his breathing and he muttered a low curse.

Not now. He couldn't afford this now. Neither of them could afford this. He shivered, abruptly as cold as he had been hot only moments ago. He wanted a cigarette. He couldn't remember the last time he'd wanted anything so badly. But he couldn't risk the light being seen. In the blackness of the jungle, even a tiny point of light would stand out, if there was anyone to see it.

Cally stirred in her sleep. He'd been hard on her. Too hard. He didn't have to see her face to know that she'd been hurt when he snapped at her. He shouldn't have snapped like that. But the thought was fuzzy around the edges. He was tired. So tired. If only he weren't so cold. No, now he was too hot.

He *would not* get sick.

Cally was barely awake when they started out again the next morning. Ryder had shaken her out of sleep to face yet another day in the apparently endless jungle. If she'd hoped that his mood might have improved overnight, she was disappointed. In the gray-green light of dawn, his face was set and hard. Unrevealing. He handed her another chunk of dried beef and a tortilla. Oh, for some bacon and eggs!

Ryder was not eating and she didn't know if it was because he'd already eaten or because he couldn't face another meal of tortillas and dried beef. His closed expression made her decide not to ask. Her mouth tasted as moldy as the food and she rinsed it with a mouthful of water, scrubbing her finger over her teeth, wishing in vain for a toothbrush and some good old Gleem. It was the little things in life that were underappreciated, she decided as she spat out the water. Ryder watched without comment, his eyes narrowed against the smoke of a cigarette.

They traveled throughout the morning without speaking. Ryder had withdrawn, warning her off without words. She didn't know if it was the incident with José that had caused his abrupt distance or if he was just distracted by the basic problems of survival.

She had no way of knowing what time it was but she guessed it to be somewhere around noon when he called a halt.

"We'll stop for lunch here. I think we've managed to lose Tomás and his merry band but I don't want to stop anywhere for long." His voice seemed more breathless than usual but then Cally felt pretty breathless herself.

He handed her the food and then sat back to

light himself a cigarette. He waved her away when she would have handed him some of the beef. The tortillas were too far gone to be edible.

"I'm not hungry." She tucked the beef back in its packaging before biting into her own portion. Her eyes drifted to Ryder. He was leaning back against a tree trunk, eyes closed. The only sign of life, the regular rise and fall of the hand that held the cigarette. Sweat trickled off his face. Her eyes sharpened. Was he pale or was it the peculiar light on the forest floor?

"Are you all right?"

His eyes snapped open, catching her in a brilliant blue stare. "Of course I'm all right." The snap in his voice dared her to suggest otherwise and Cally backed down, shaking her head slightly. He was certainly in a foul mood. She quickly swallowed the last of the beef as he got to his feet.

"There's a river not too far ahead. I want to get there before nightfall."

"Okay." Cally ignored the protests of her aching muscles and nodded her agreement. A river at least promised to break up the monotony of endless jungle. Besides, the quicker the pace they maintained, the quicker she'd get back to civilization. And the quicker she'd say good-bye to Ryder Allen. Which was all for the better, she assured herself, trying not to wince as a tiny lizard darted out from under her feet.

It would be too easy to think that she was attracted to him, even to think that there might be something more between them than a relationship

155

based strictly on circumstance. Just because her heart had seemed to swell when he told José that he loved her more than life itself, that didn't mean it was because she wished it were true. It was just the tension of the moment.

Ahead of her, Ryder stumbled, catching himself with a hand against a tree trunk. It was the first time Cally had seen him miss his step among all the vines and debris on the forest floor. He didn't pause and the set of his back made it impossible for her to say anything.

They reached the river in the late afternoon. It was broad and slow moving, a movie set full of alligators and piranhas. Ryder stopped a few yards away, staying in the shadow of the forest, scanning the relatively clear bank for any sign of life. Sunlight glittered on the water and Cally thought she'd never seen a more exotically beautiful setting in her life. The forest looming dark and ominous along the banks and the water floating along so peacefully. She slapped absently at a mosquito that was trying to drain all the blood from her body.

"Wait here." Ryder's voice was husky, tired. Stealing a glance at his face, she thought again that he looked pale.

He edged out of the forest and moved slowly down the slope to the river. He knelt down and filled their two canteens. Cally tried not to think of what might lurk in the river. Water was water and, once it was treated, it might not taste good but it would keep them alive.

He knelt by the bank longer than was necessary

and the thought slipped into her mind that he was gathering his strength to stand up. She dismissed it quickly. He couldn't be ill. If something happened to him, they were both dead. She was no helpless flower but she couldn't get them out of the jungle. Not alone. She held her breath as he stood up, trying not to think that he seemed to have trouble getting up.

He walked back up the bank toward her and Cally noticed that sweat was pouring off him. There was a slightly unfocused look in his eyes but they sharpened quickly enough when he saw her watching him.

"We didn't get rain yesterday but it won't miss today. There's a cave not too far from here. We can shelter there until the rain stops and then get in a few more miles before dark."

It wasn't far to the cave he'd mentioned. Back into the jungle a few yards and then they paralleled the river. The ground began to climb slowly and Cally could no longer pretend that something wasn't wrong. Ryder stumbled and would have fallen if he hadn't grabbed hold of a thick vine that hung from one of the trees. He jerked his hand back with a pained exclamation and stared at his palm. Cally hurried to his side, taking his hand to examine the puncture wounds that marched across his palm. The vine was covered with a heavy layer of long thorns and several of them had broken off in his flesh. She started to try and pick them out but he stopped her.

His other hand closed over her shoulder, the fingers biting down. She glanced up into his face and forgot about the relatively minor problem of his hand. Something was very wrong. Sweat beaded his forehead and his skin had an unhealthy grayish cast that wasn't caused by the peculiar jungle light. His eyes were bright. Too bright, she realized. Feverishly bright.

"What's wrong?"

"I'm just tired. That's all. Just tired." The words were slurred and obviously untrue but she didn't argue with him.

"Let me help you. We'll get you to this cave and you can rest. But you'll have to show me where the cave is."

"Rest. That's all I need. Just a few hours' rest." She slipped her shoulder under his arm, bracing herself to help support his weight.

"Ryder, you'll have to show me where the cave is." She made her voice sharp, trying not to think of what she was going to do if he was too far gone to tell her that much. She felt the shiver that went through him. She could sense the effort he was making to pull his thoughts into order.

"I'm all right." His voice was clear but he didn't pull away from her support. She'd never been quite so painfully aware of the disadvantages of being small as she was during the time it took them to find the cave. Though he clearly tried to support as much of his weight as possible, he leaned heavily on her slender frame. Twice he stumbled and she was sure that this time she would surely collapse under his weight. Each time, she summoned strength she didn't know she had and managed to keep them upright.

The mouth of the cave was shielded by vines that covered the rock wall above and she almost sobbed with relief when she finally found it. She wanted to stagger inside and collapse but some vague instinct told her that she should check to make sure the cave was unoccupied first. She propped Ryder against the rock wall next to the opening and tugged the pistol he'd given her out of her waistband.

Ryder watched through foggy vision as she crept toward the entrance, gun ready. He smiled vaguely at the picture she made. Did she think that pistol was going to stop a jaguar if one was denning in the cave? The thought of Cally facing a jaguar snapped him out of the fever induced stupor and he struggled upright, slipping the rifle off his shoulder. The gun seemed to weigh too much, but he forced his fingers around the stock and stepped away from the wall.

The ground showed a disconcerting tendency to shift beneath him but, if he concentrated, he could walk an almost steady line. He was supposed to be protecting Cally. She shouldn't be going into the cave alone. He was supposed to be protecting her.

The brief spurt of strength faded as he tried to duck beneath the trailing vines. His legs started to buckle and he would have fallen if Cally's shoulder hadn't suddenly been beneath his arm, bracing him.

"I told you to stay put," she told him as she

guided his staggering footsteps deeper into the shallow cave.

"Protecting you." The words were slurred, almost indistinguishable.

"You've done a great job of protecting me. Now just let me take care of you for a little while." She refused to let her voice show any uncertainty. She eased him down onto the floor of the cave.

His hand caught her wrist with surprising strength when she moved to stand up. His eyes burned into hers and she read frustration and desperation in the bright blue depths.

"I'm just tired. I'll be all right in the morning." The words were strong but their impact was destroyed by the shiver that racked him as soon as he quit speaking.

"Nobody said you wouldn't be all right in the morning." She spoke automatically, giving him the words she knew he wanted to hear. "But right now you need to get some rest. Don't worry about anything. I'll take care of everything."

Ryder's last vision was of her eyes, a calm gray, steady on his as he slid into unconsciousness.

CHAPTER NINE

"No! You can't die! I won't let you. NO!"

Cally came awake, heart pounding. She'd fallen asleep. She hadn't planned on falling asleep at all. For a few seconds she was disoriented and then Ryder's voice came again, a low rasp that tore at her heart.

"Joe. Don't die. Don't leave me here alone." There was an uncertain, youthful quality in the tones, at odds with the husky tones she was accustomed to.

She groped her way forward in the darkness, putting her hand on his shoulder. He reacted instantly, his hand closing over hers, almost crushing her slender fingers.

"Joe?"

"It's Cally, Ryder. Cally."

She heard him stir restlessly, as if disturbed. His hand tightened for a moment and she gasped in pain. "Joe." The name was a confirmation and then his hold loosened and he seemed to slip into sleep.

She sat back against the wall, rubbing her fingers absently. What was she going to do? She had no idea where Ryder had been going and it wouldn't mean anything to her if she did know. She'd always been reasonably self-sufficient—her upbringing had seen to that—but there was no way she could find her way out of the jungle.

Despite his claims that he was just tired, it was easy to see that he was sick. How sick she couldn't even begin to guess. She could only hope that he had enough lucid moments for her to find out if he knew what was wrong with him. As soon as there was enough light to see, she would go through his pack and see if there was anything in there that resembled a first-aid kit. She had the feeling that whatever was wrong with him, it was something he was familiar with. Maybe he had some medication with him.

She closed her eyes, knowing there was little she could do until dawn. As it turned out, there was little she could do after dawn either. There was a first-aid kit in the pack but it didn't contain anything more than the standard-issue equipment, nothing that would lower the fever that raged through Ryder.

She treated the hand he'd injured the day before, feeling as if she were patching a pinpoint hole in the dike while a crack threatened to split wide open. But there was nothing she could do for his fever and she could do something for his hand.

"How long have I been out?" Cally jumped, dropping the tube of antiseptic cream she'd been putting away. Her eyes flew to his face. His gaze was feverishly bright but it was coherent. She put her hand on his forehead, feeling the heat that burned in him.

"Just since last night. What's wrong with you? What should I do?"

"You can't do anything. Just let it run its course." He shut his eyes, exhausted by the small effort, and Cally was afraid he'd passed out again. His hand came up to catch hers, his hold weak, but she sensed the urgency in him.

"Cally, Tomás is still going to be looking for us." He had to stop for breath and she tried to reassure him.

"I know. I don't think they're likely to find this cave and I'll be careful."

"No, you've got to leave me here and go on." His fingers tightened, cutting off her automatic protest and he opened his eyes, letting her see the urgency he didn't have the breath to express. "In my pocket there's a roll of film. It has to get out. Take it and the compass. Follow the river and where it veers south, keep going due east. There's a village. Not far. Wait there. Someone will come."

"Ryder, I'm not going to leave you here alone."

His mouth stretched in a ghost of a smile, apparently trying to reassure her. "I'll be all right. I'll just wait for this to pass and then join you."

"Ryder . . ."

"Promise me you'll go." His breathing was rapid, harsh and, without a moment's hesitation Cally gave him the promise he wanted.

"I'll go." She saw the relief in his eyes and de-

163

cided that the lie was worth the small twinge of conscience. "Ryder, how long does this last?" But he'd already slipped back into unconsciousness.

She sat back on her heels and studied him, trying not to think of how frightened she was. She'd been depending on him to keep her alive ever since she'd realized he wasn't going to hurt her. Now, here she was, alone in the middle of the jungle, with an entire guerrilla army looking for them. She had no idea where they were or just how far away help might be. Ryder was ill and had no one to care for him but her. She only hoped she could take care of him half as well as he cared for her.

The next three days were a nightmare. Ryder had only momentary spells of coherency bordered by long periods of unconsciousness and delirium. The first day was not too bad. She coaxed him to eat and managed to get plenty of water down him. He seemed only vaguely aware that she was there. Late in the afternoon, she helped him outside so that he could go to the bathroom and he showed a momentary flash of his usual strength when he insisted that he was perfectly capable of managing that much on his own. She hovered by the mouth of the cave, counting the seconds and debating how long she should wait before going to see if he'd collapsed. The moment he stepped into sight, she hurried to his side, and it was a measure of his weakness that he didn't even attempt to push away her supporting arm.

Cally spent two hours before dark rigging up a

way to hang one of the blankets across the mouth of the cave so that she could light a fire. With careful maneuvering, she even managed to position the fire so that the smoke drifted out through a gap at the top of the blanket. Slipping outside into the pitch blackness, she reassured herself that the light could not be seen from outside.

It was time well spent because, with nightfall, his fever worsened. Without the light of the fire, she could never have managed. She bathed his forehead and tried to keep him covered, praying that she was doing the right things. She heated water over the fire and made broth from the supplies he'd dug up and all but force-fed him to get some of it down him.

She caught snatches of sleep during the moments when he seemed to be sleeping. He was delirious much of the time, sometimes muttering incoherently, once or twice shouting out in apparent fear or pain. From what she could piece together, he was having flashbacks to time he'd spent in Vietnam, another jungle and someone named Joe.

By the time he settled into sleep, Cally was near tears from sheer exhaustion. Taking stock of their supplies, she knew she would have to make a trip to the river for more water. It was important that he not become dehydrated. But that meant leaving him alone.

She closed her eyes. She would catch a couple of hours of sleep and then consider the problem. Right now, she was too tired to think out a solution. When she opened her eyes, the fire was out and weak sunlight oozed through the blanket that shielded the entrance. She yawned. When she looked at Ryder, she saw that his eyes were open and aware.

"You're supposed to be gone." His voice was hardly more than a whisper.

Cally laid her hand on his forehead. It was still too warm but was it just wishful thinking that made it seem cooler than it had been?

"I'm not leaving you here."

"I told you I'd be all right."

"I know what you told me. I'm not leaving you here."

He closed his eyes as if the effort of keeping them open was just too great. "Stubborn."

"So I've been told." She brushed the hair back from his forehead. "Ryder, we need more water. I'm going to go down to the river and get some. Will you be all right on your own?"

"I'm fine." The breathlessness of the words reduced their impact. "Help me outside." He started to struggle up on one elbow and Cally moved automatically to aid him. Sweat coated his brow and he had to stop to get his breath once he was sitting upright.

"Ryder, you're not well enough for this. Let me . . ."

His eyes opened and pinned her, traces of temper in their depths. "I am going to go outside and go to the bathroom and I don't need you telling me what I am and am not well enough to do. I'm not an invalid!" He stopped, his breathing ragged.

Cally said nothing. Talk about stubborn. If awards were handed out for sheer pigheadedness, he would certainly win the grand prize. She didn't say a word, even when she had to almost drag him back into the cave and help him collapse on the sleeping bag. What little color he'd had was gone and his skin seemed stretched across his cheekbones, giving him the hollow look of a cadaver. He opened his eyes, daring her to say anything, but Cally wouldn't have commented if her life depended on it.

"I'll wait till this afternoon to go get water. We've got enough to last until then. I'm going to make you some soup. You need to keep your strength up as much as possible."

He watched while she heated water and dumped a packet of soup mix into it. She poured the broth into a metal cup and brought it over to him. He grudgingly accepted her help in sitting up but took the mug from her, muttering that he was more than capable of feeding himself. Cally watched without comment, waiting until he'd spilled it on himself for the second time before she took the mug from him. He was too tired to bother with more than a weak glare as she held the mug to his mouth while he sipped.

"How long do these spells usually last?" She eased him back down onto the sleeping bag as she spoke.

Ryder closed his eyes and shook his head. "Two, three days. Sometimes as much as a week. I

wish you'd just take the film and leave me alone."
But he was asleep with the words.

Cally brushed the thick black hair from his fore-head, feeling her heart ache at his suffering. The heavy black shadow on his jaw emphasized his pallor and gave him a strangely defenseless look. He looked much younger than his thirty-eight years. Young and helpless. And lovable.

She shook her head, refusing to pursue that line of thinking. Too dangerous. The circumstances were extraordinary. Shared dangers would make it easy to think that they were closer than they really were.

Her fingers traced the line of his mustache, marveling at its softness, remembering the feel of it against her mouth. No one had ever kissed her and made her feel as if nothing else mattered. She'd always thought that those kinds of feelings were mere figments of writers' imaginations. But at the same time it had always seemed that something was missing when a man kissed her and she felt nothing but mild pleasure. Who would have thought that she'd find that kind of wild excitement in the midst of a Central American jungle with a man who was about as tough as they came?

She drew her fingers away from his mouth. There was no sense in trying to analyze their relationship. She'd probably find that once they were back in civilization he would hold no appeal for her at all. The thought seemed remarkably hollow and she acknowledged that, in civilization or not, there was no way that John Ryder Allen would ever be anything less than magnetic.

Ryder slept most of the day, stirring restlessly and muttering in his sleep but not really waking. Cally sorted out their food supplies, calculating that if the fever lasted a week they would have less than a week to reach the village he'd spoken of. But the fever wasn't going to last a week, she told herself bracingly. He'd said it was usually only two or three days. She was going to count on that estimate being correct.

It was late afternoon when she checked on him one final time and then slipped out of the cave. The river flowed below them, serene and quiet. All she had to do was negotiate the jungle that lay between here and there, fill the canteens, and return. Sounded simple enough. If she could just avoid stepping on a fer-de-lance or bumping into one of the rarely seen jaguars or falling into the river to be devoured by piranhas or alligators. Piece of cake.

She drew a deep breath and crept into the jungle. She reached the river without incident, unless you counted being frightened into near heart attack when a huge butterfly fluttered from out of nowhere and flew right into her face. She filled the canteens and stood up, only to drop almost flat on her face when a voice spoke from out of nowhere.

"This is a good place for a camp." There was an indistinguishable reply and then the first voice spoke again. "They are long gone, amigo. It is only Tomás's pride that keeps us out here looking."

Cally flattened herself into the dank vegetation that lined the river. For once, she didn't even wonder about the insect life that undoubtedly teemed beneath her. Tomás's men! Damn! What was she supposed to do now? She couldn't lie here like a slug waiting for them to find her. And Ryder wasn't going to come to her rescue this time. He lay helpless in the cave.

"Me, I'm not so sure we want to find them anyway." Again that indistinguishable murmur. And then the first voice. "Rico is quiet but the quiet ones are dangerous. I do not wish to face that knife of his. And he knows the jungles better than any gringo has a right to. He could probably sneak up and slit your throat before you even knew he was there."

Cally almost smiled. He made Ryder sound like the main character in an adventure story. But the amusement was brief. She had to figure a way to get back to the cave without being seen. She wiggled forward on her belly, the canteens bumping painfully against her sides. If she could make it to that huge palm, she might be able to slip from tree to tree and work her way around them. It wasn't going to get any easier if she waited.

By the time she slipped into the cave, she felt as if she'd aged twenty years. If there'd been a mirror to show that her hair had gone from silver and gold to steel gray, she wouldn't have been surprised. She just wasn't cut out for this spy business. Slipping through the jungle, waiting for the shout that said she'd been discovered—things like that were all very exciting in a movie but they were painfully unpleasant to experience.

The night that followed made all the days that had passed seem like child's play. Ryder slipped further into delirium. Tossing and turning, seeing people that weren't there, reliving events long past. Vividly aware of Tomás's men camped so close, Cally was terrified that he was going to cry out and reveal their presence.

"Ryder, please. You've got to be quiet or they'll find us." Her voice broke on a sob.

His eyes suddenly snapped open, focusing on something only he could see. In the flickering firelight, he looked half mad. "Joe? Is it the Cong? Are they close?"

"Yes. You have to be quiet or they'll find us."

"Where's my gun? Did we lose it in the crash?"

"Don't worry about it. I have your gun. You're hurt but I'll take care of you. Just lie still."

Cally held her breath, praying that the words would get through to him. He lay tense beneath her hands for a moment and then collapsed back against the makeshift bed. "You're just a kid. Should be home playing baseball."

"Don't worry about me. I'm okay."

"Just a kid. Shouldn't be here. Sorry about the crash. My fault."

He closed his eyes, his head tossing as he fell back into incoherent mumblings. Cally's hand was shaking as she dampened a cloth and passed it over his forehead.

He couldn't have been much more than a kid

himself when he was in 'Nam. Who was Joe and what had happened to him? Whatever it was, it had obviously been preying on Ryder's subconscious all these years.

By dawn, Cally was exhausted. She fell asleep lying on the cave floor next to Ryder, one arm thrown across his chest as if that light weight might hold him down. The following forty-eight hours repeated the same cycle endlessly. The only change was that a cautious reconnaissance told her that Tomás's men had left the area.

The third night, his fever climbed until she was sure that his body couldn't possibly contain the heat that raged through him. He tossed and turned, shouting and mumbling. She no longer had the strength to even try to follow his ramblings. All she could do was bathe his face and pray for the fever to break. Sometime before dawn she dozed off sitting against the wall of the cave. When she woke, first light was seeping through the doorway of vines and blanket.

Ryder lay beside her, absolutely still. She stared at him, eyes wide with fright. For a moment, she couldn't detect any movement, not even the rise and fall of his chest. She put her hand to his chest, relieved when she felt the shallow beat of his heart. But why was he so still? Had he slipped into a coma? Her breath caught on a sob as she laid her palm on his forehead. She was so tired that it took a moment for her to take in the significance of what she was feeling. His skin was cool and damp. Cool. It was cool.

The fever had broken.

A sob slipped out, followed by another and then another. She slid down onto the floor, letting her palm rest on the wonderfully cool surface of his chest, right over the steady beat of his heart. She closed her eyes and fell into a deep heavy sleep, the tears still wet on her cheeks.

Ryder came awake slowly, as if swimming up out of a pool of lead. He felt heavy, groggy, his thoughts fuzzy. He opened his eyes on bare rock walls. He frowned, trying to remember. The cave and Cally.

Cally. He turned his head with a monumental effort. She lay sprawled out on the hard floor next to him, her arm thrown over his chest, her hair trailing in the dust. Her skin was as pale as he felt, dark smudges beneath her eyes testifying to too many days with too little sleep.

He shut his eyes again, piecing together what he could remember of the past few days. How many days? He didn't know. There had been flashes of coherency. He'd told Cally to take the film and leave and she'd refused. He remembered her feeding him, helping him outside. And Joe had been there. No, that wasn't possible. That must have been the nightmares. Joe had been dead for fifteen years.

He opened his eyes. How long had the fever lasted? He shifted, grimacing at the sticky, dirty feel of his body. He must smell like a boar hog in June. It took a huge effort to lift his hand and shift

173

Cally's arm from his chest. It was an even greater effort to sit up. Once that was accomplished, he could only lean back against the wall of the cave and curse his weakness.

Damn this fever. He was sweating like a pig. His mouth twisted. Smelling like a boar. Sweating like a pig. The fever seemed to have left him with a lot of comparisons about swine.

His eyes drifted to Cally who hadn't moved an inch. One hand lay across the space where he'd been, the other was tucked under her cheek, providing a pillow. She looked amazingly young and fragile. But enough memories survived of the past few days to tell him that she'd managed to hold things together with a strength that belied that fragile appearance.

He reached out to brush the hair back from her face. His fingers shook slightly with weakness and he allowed them to linger against the soft skin of her cheek. There was a slight fuzziness to her cheek, reminding him of babies and rose petals, things that had no place in his world.

He pulled his hand back, pushing the thoughts from his mind. The sooner he regained his strength, the better. He was getting soft in the head.

So it was that Cally opened her eyes to his frown. She hardly noticed. All that concerned her was that he was sitting up, obviously no longer gripped by fever. She scrambled to her knees.

"How are you feeling?" Her palm came out to

174

touch his forehead but he winced away, the frown deepening.

"Like hell. How long have I been out of it?"

"Three, four days. I've kind of lost track. It must be four days because Tomás's men showed up on the second day and that was two nights ago."

"Tomás's men? Where are they? Did they see you?"

"They left and I assume they didn't see me because I'm still here to talk to you." She grinned, not even caring that he was in a grumpy mood. He was awake and sane and on the mend. Nothing else mattered.

"Thank God. We've got to get moving. We've been here too long as it is."

"I don't think you're going to be ready to travel for a few days," she cautioned.

"I'll be ready to travel this afternoon." He stood up, shooting her a ferocious scowl when he was forced to use her support to get to his feet. Cally wanted to throw her arms around him and hug him but she was wise enough not to do that.

Ryder's mood did not improve when Cally's estimate proved to be a lot closer than his. The first day, it was all he could do to walk outside. He was able to feed himself but the effort left him weak and drained and he slept most of the afternoon.

Cally could feel his mood deteriorating with each passing hour. He didn't snap at her. He accepted her help with muttered thanks but she could feel the tension building in him. He absolutely hated the fact that the tables had turned and

175

he had to depend on her. Cally watched the tension build in him, feeling a corresponding tension in herself.

Sooner or later, his temper was going to snap and the explosion was bound to be devastating.

CHAPTER TEN

The fire crackled with a cheerful sound that was at odds with the tension between the cave's occupants. Cally felt like a rubber band being twisted tighter and tighter. Stealing a glance at Ryder, she could see the lines that bracketed his mustache were carved deep into his cheeks. With a silent exhalation, she dropped her eyes. It was a lot like being trapped with a tiger. You knew that sooner or later the tiger was going to pounce, you just didn't know when.

"We'll leave tomorrow morning." The silence was so complete that Ryder's husky voice startled her into dropping the comb. She picked it up again, dusting it on the leg of her jeans.

"Are you sure you're up to it?"

"Yes, I'm sure I'm up to it." The snap in the words brought a hint of moisture to her eyes but she willed it back, bending her head forward and pulling the comb through her hair. He wasn't really snapping at her, he was furious with the situation.

Silence filled the small cave again. The blanket

177

cut them off from the black, silent jungle outside. There might have been nothing in the world but this cavern; no one but the two of them. Cally pulled the comb through her hair, unconsciously picking up the rhythm of Ryder's knife stroking across the whetstone.

Ryder lifted the knife from the whetstone, testing its edge with his thumb before slipping it back in its sheath. His eyes were drawn to the hypnotic motion of the comb through her hair. When she tossed the heavy length back, the ends of it trailed the ground behind her. In the firelight, it gleamed like a precious metal, shining and lustrous, inviting a man to run his fingers through it. She began to stroke the comb through it again, eyes dreamy.

What was she thinking of? Strange that, in some ways, he knew so little about her. Was there a boy-friend back in the States? Was that why her eyes had that soft, unfocused look? There was a sharp pain in his chest and it took him a moment to realize that it was pure unadulterated jealousy. The realization caught him off guard and he felt betrayed by his own emotions.

His hands clenched into fists. He wanted to bury his fingers in her hair and pull her to him. He wanted to feel her mouth soften under his. He wanted to drive out any memories of any other man she'd ever kissed. He closed his eyes, fighting back the urges, the needs.

Cally looked up to see his face tight with pain, eyes closed, white lines around his mouth. Her only thought was that he was in some kind of pain.

Perhaps something that he'd been hiding from her all along. She was across the narrow space that separated them before the thought was complete.

"Ryder? What's wrong?"

His eyes snapped open on her concerned face. She was so close. Mere inches separated them. The faint herbal smell of soap mingled with the woodsy scent of the fire. He could see the thrust of her breasts beneath the fabric of his shirt. His shirt. That she was wearing something of his seemed suddenly very intimate.

"I'm fine." He got the words out between gritted teeth, fighting the confusing mixture of anger, need, and desire that boiled in him.

"Are you sure? You look pale. You don't have a fever again, do you?" She lifted her hand and the feel of her palm on his forehead was sweet agony. Ryder closed his eyes, gathering anger around him as a defense against other, more dangerous emotions.

"Would you stop trying to mother me!" Cally pulled her hand back as if scalded.

"I was just—"

"I don't need or want you hovering over me." His voice rose with the accumulated tension of days, of months of living on the edge. "I'd probably have recovered a lot faster if it hadn't been for your damned coddling!"

This was patently unfair but Cally had been under a lot of pressure too. Her own temper was less than stable and it built with every word, every decibel his voice climbed.

"I should have left you alone just to see how well you managed. You'd have starved to death if the fever didn't kill you or Tomás's men didn't find you first. I don't know why I almost killed myself trying to keep you quiet when they were here. I should have let them find you. You're pigheaded, nasty, hard to get along with and an ingrate and I don't know how I ever thought I could be in love with you!"

Her voice rose with every sentence and the last was just under a shout. There was a moment of stunned silence. The fire popped, the sound like a gunshot in the stillness. Cally's eyes met Ryder's for an instant before skidding away.

"You're hardly more than a child. You don't even know the meaning of the word love."

The condescending tone sparked her temper again. How dare he call her a child and act as if she didn't know her own mind?

"You're so afraid of committing yourself that you're hardly qualified to judge."

Stung, his voice carried a snap. "I've spent almost a year in this damn jungle doing a job. I think that's a commitment."

She waved one hand in a contemptuous gesture of dismissal. "A job. That's not hard to commit yourself to. But you're scared to death of making any commitment to another human being. That's probably why you've got a job like this. It's easier to play super-spy than it is to try and function in the real world. You wouldn't recognize love if it ran up and bit you on the nose."

The truth of the words shot through Ryder, angering him, frightening him. His hands shot out to catch her by the shoulders, pulling her off balance so that she fell against his chest. He caught a glimpse of the startled gray of her eyes before his mouth came down on hers, cutting off any protest she might have made.

If he'd stopped to analyze his actions, he would have said that he'd planned to scare her, to punish her, to prove to her that she knew nothing about love. If he'd dug still deeper into his muddled motivations, he'd have admitted that he was also punishing himself, tasting forbidden fruit, torturing himself with what he could never have.

If Cally had struggled, he'd have released her. If she'd been passive, he'd have been able to pull his hands away from her and set her away, feeling that he'd proved to her that love was not the pretty emotion she thought it was. If she'd done any of the expected things, it would have ended right there.

But she didn't do the expected. When his mouth touched hers, she froze for an instant and then her hands came up—not to push him away but to slip into the thick blackness of his hair, pulling him still closer. Her mouth opened beneath his, inviting —no, demanding—that the kiss deepen. She seemed to explode in his arms, catching his defenses down. All the confused motivations for kissing her vanished like wisps of smoke beneath the hard surge of desire that swept through him.

His arms tightened until she was crushed

against his chest. His tongue slipped into the welcoming cavern of her mouth. She was every dream he'd ever had and she was more than he could have dreamed.

Cally's fingers wound deeper into his hair, feeling it slide through her fingers like midnight silk. His beard rasped against her skin, contrasting with the softer brush of his mustache. The heat that rose in her body was something new. She wanted to stop and savor the moment, explore the new sensations but there was no time. She was driven by an urgency as great as what drove him.

He twisted and she was suddenly looking up at him. The sleeping bag was beneath her but she wouldn't have noticed had it been a bed of nails. Ryder's shoulders were outlined by the faint firelight. Cally's hands came up to flatten against the hair of his chest, pushing the open shirt off his shoulders.

The feel of her hands on his body, the open desire in her eyes, the sight of her lying beneath him —eager, wanting—everything combined to fulfill his fantasies. Fantasies he'd been afraid to even acknowledge.

She felt the groan that rumbled in his chest, caught the fire in his eyes before he lowered his body to cover hers. When she'd thought about it, she'd always thought passion would be a more gentle emotion, seeping through her body, making her languid with desire. She'd never imagined the way it burned under her skin, making her feel feverish, hungry, demanding. She'd never pictured her skin becoming so sensitive that every touch was almost painful in the intensity of feeling it brought.

Her fingers twined in his hair, pulling his mouth to hers, her lips parting to invite the hungry thrust of his tongue. Her clothes seemed to slide from her beneath the impatient demands of his fingers. She was equally impatient with his clothing, fumbling with zippers and buttons that seemed determined to frustrate her. Ryder made no effort to help. With her lying bare beneath him, he was intent on savoring every silken inch of skin.

Cally's hands left his waistband to clench against his waist, her breath leaving her in a startled gasp as his mouth found the gentle swell of her breast. His beard brushed lightly across the tender flesh, sensitizing the skin, preparing it for the hot moisture of his tongue. His lips closed around one swollen peak and she felt the drawing sensation at her breast and also deep in her womb, tugging at the heavy liquid weight that had settled there.

His hands slid down her body to her hips, his knee slipping between her thighs as he drew her closer. The khaki fabric of his pants was stretched taut over the strong muscles of his leg and Cally gasped as he pressed against her in a delicate rocking motion. Her short nails bit into his skin, her head fell back and she gave herself over to the dual demands of his mouth and the pressure of his knee. He moved his attention to her other breast, bringing up one hand to gently stroke the nipple.

"Please." The word moaned between her clenched teeth. "Please."

His teeth gently scored her nipple at the same time that his knee pressed deeper. She whimpered, feeling need burning through her body. Her hands moved to his waist, struggling with the recalcitrant zipper. She needed to feel him against her. Her fingers were shaking and she whimpered in frustration.

"Shh." His breath whispered out over her breast. She almost cried out when he pulled away from her clinging hands, standing up in the small confines of the cave, his body silhouetted against the firelight as he stripped off his clothing. Cally wondered if it was only the firelight that made him seem bathed in a golden glow, his skin gleaming like a bronzed statue.

He knelt in front of her, struggling for some semblance of self-control. He hadn't intended for this to happen. This wasn't what he wanted. His hands came to rest on the firm planes of her stomach. She was so warm. A flame that drew him closer. This was insane.

"This is crazy." He was hardly aware of muttering the words out loud. His hands were sliding upward to cup the gentle weight of her breasts.

Cally's eyes glittered with an invitation as old as time. One slender hand reached out to close around him, feeling the burning heat of his arousal.

"Then we're both crazy." Her husky voice shivered over him, smothering the thin voice of sanity.

"Please, Ryder. Don't make me wait any longer." Her hand tightened, drawing a groan from him.

He lowered himself over her, his knees sliding between her legs, opening her to him. He braced himself on his elbows, careful not to crush her slim form beneath his weight.

"Madness." He whispered the word against her mouth. Their eyes locked as his hips lowered. Her pupils widened at the first feeling of him against the softest part of her. Ryder could not drag his gaze from hers as he deepened the contact, feeling the damp velvet of her enclosing him, inviting him. He saw the flicker of hesitation in her eyes at the same moment he felt resistance to his possession. His eyes widened in shock and his body tensed but it was too late. Far too late to stop now.

"Hold on." He ground the words out between his teeth, his mouth coming down on hers as his body flexed forward. His lips caught her shallow gasp of pain, making it his own.

Cally lay still beneath him, absorbing the sensation of sharing her body with a man. The first twinge of pain faded quickly to be replaced by a wonderful feeling of completion and an urgency, a knowledge that there was something more lying ahead.

Ryder waited until he felt her hands relax against his back and then he began to move. Slowly, so slowly, letting her pick up the rhythm. Never in his life had he exercised such control. His body burned with the need to rush headlong to fulfillment. Sweat beaded his forehead as he forced himself to a slow pace, coaxing her along the path with him.

Cally twisted restlessly, hungrily, aching with feelings that were new and urgent. Madness, he'd said. And he was right. She felt mad. Her hands slid up and down his back, tracing every sweat-dampened muscle. Her head tossed back and forth, scattering her hair across the dark fabric of the sleeping bag. The tension that was building deep in her belly threatened to explode. She tensed, half-frightened of the intensity of that feeling, but Ryder wouldn't let her back away from the final experience.

"Come with me. Don't stop now." The words were half-coaxing, half-demand. He wound his fingers in her hair, forcing her to meet his eyes as he slowed the rhythm of their lovemaking.

Cally felt as if she were falling into the brilliant blue of his eyes, absorbed in the demands he was making. She arched beneath him, suddenly anxious to take the final steps.

The pace increased and Cally fell headlong into the madness. Her body arched beneath him, taut as a bowstring, caught in shuddering pleasure. He groaned as the delicate contractions snatched at the lingering remnants of his control, pulling him with her into the swirling vortex of fulfillment.

It was a long time before either of them moved and she groaned a protest as he lifted himself from her and rolled to the side. He sat up and reached out to put a small stick on the fire that provided

186

the only source of illumination. When he didn't lie back down, Cally opened her eyes reluctantly.

Ryder was lighting a cigarette with a twig taken from the fire, his eyes narrowed against the smoke as he inhaled and tossed the twig back into the flames. With one elbow propped on an updrawn knee, the fire flickering behind him, he looked surprisingly aloof for a man without a stitch of clothing.

"I guess all those rumors about a man always smoking afterward are true." She bit her lip as soon as the flip remark was out. She sounded young and nervous and inexperienced. It wasn't the sophisticated woman-of-the-world attitude he was probably accustomed to.

"You were a virgin." The flat statement was impossible to analyze and Cally didn't know if he was angry, pleased, surprised, or just making polite conversation.

She sat up, reaching for her shirt. She felt at a distinct disadvantage and the thin shield offered by the cotton shirt was appealing. She struggled to turn the sleeves right side out, striving for a light voice.

"Surprise! I guess I forgot to tell you that." His hand caught hold of the shirt just as she'd succeeded in getting it untangled. She stared down at the tanned fingers wrapped around the fabric, denying her the false courage that came with being covered.

"You should have told me." Again the tone was flat, unrevealing.

"It's not exactly the kind of thing that you can bring up in polite conversation. 'Hi. I'm sorry to tell you that your friend kidnapped the wrong woman. I'm Cally Stevens not Lisa Wellington and, by the way, I happen to be a virgin.' " She stopped abruptly, aware that her voice was shaking.

Silence fell, an almost visible presence between them. Cally stared at his hand, remembering the feel of it on her body, wondering what it was that he expected her to say.

"Are you angry?" She took a deep breath and lifted her eyes to his face, searching the impassive features, trying to read what he was thinking.

"Angry?" *Yes,* he wanted to shout. He hadn't asked, didn't want the responsibility she had handed him. There were already too many ties, too many shared emotions between them. He should never have become her lover at all but, if she were an experienced woman, he could at least fool himself into thinking that that was all there was to it.

But his touch was the only touch she'd ever known. She had given him something that could never be given again. Virginity might not be prized as it had once been. It was no longer used as a bargaining chip over marriage tables, but nothing could take away the fact that it was a significant moment in a woman's life when she trusted a man enough to make love for the first time.

He didn't want her trust. It frightened him. Was he angry? He was furious. With himself. With her. With the situation. With the world that had made him what he was. Too old, too hard, too experienced. But her eyes were so wide and scared. Her hair spilled across slender shoulders, catching the firelight. Her soft mouth was swollen with his kisses, her body flushed from his lovemaking.

He tossed the half-smoked cigarette into the fire before reaching out to slip his hand around the back of her neck, his thumb brushing the sensitive spot under her ear. His mouth twisted in a smile but he was unaware of the way his eyes softened.

"I'm not angry." It was a half-truth but it was enough to ease the tension from her face. "Did I hurt you?"

She smiled shakily, letting him ease her down until they lay on the sleeping bag. Her head seemed to fit his shoulder perfectly, her body tucked neatly along his side.

"You didn't hurt me. Only a little, at first." Her fingers slid through the curls on his chest.

He couldn't resist the urge to fill his hands with the pale silk of her hair, letting it caress his fingers. But, inside, he was filled with turmoil. Emotions he didn't even want to name, let alone face.

"Why me, Cally? Why me?" He hadn't intended to voice the question aloud but now it was out and he waited for the answer.

Her hand stopped its exploration and her slim body tensed against him. After a moment, he slid his fingers under her chin and tilted her head back until he could look into her face. She bit her lip, but her eyes met his without wavering and he was suddenly sorry he'd asked the question.

"Never mind. Dumb question."

She ignored his attempt to backtrack. "I think I'm falling in love with you."

He closed his eyes, not wanting to see the openness of her expression, afraid of the rush of emotion her words brought. When he opened his eyes, she was still looking at him with that total lack of guile that made him feel so defenseless. Uneasy, he dropped his gaze to her mouth, concentrating on the sweet curve of it.

"It's late. We should try and get some sleep before morning. With any luck, we can make the village before nightfall tomorrow."

Cally let her head fall back on his shoulder, swallowing a twinge of disappointment. She hadn't expected him to raise the flag and declare his love for her but she'd hoped for some reaction. She closed her eyes as his arm tightened around her, pulling her closer to his lean body, leaving room for nothing larger than a shadow to slip between them. She half-smiled. Perhaps she should let his actions speak. He held her so close. Maybe that was the only answer she needed for now.

When Cally woke the next morning, she was aware of an immediate feeling of something being different. She lay still, exploring the new awareness in her body. She was a bit sore—more a tenderness than an actual discomfort. But beyond that was a feeling of unfamiliarity. She stretched without opening her eyes, feeling wonderfully sensuous.

Her nose twitched with the scent of coffee and

she opened her eyes slowly, reluctant to admit that she was awake. Ryder crouched next to the small fire. In front of him was a pot, gently steaming and sending off the heavenly scent that had awakened her.

He was shoeless and shirtless, his pants zipped but not snapped. His hands were wrapped around an aluminum mug but his eyes were on her, cobalt blue and hungry. Cally lay frozen for a moment, almost frightened of the intensity in his look. His eyes dropped away to skim over her body and she felt a flush start at her toes and work its way to the top of her head. It was one thing to make love with him, but the golden firelight of the night before was very different from the broad daylight that spilled in through the vines at the mouth of the cave.

If Ryder sensed her embarrassment, he didn't give any sign. His eyes didn't shift away, even when she sat up and reached for her shirt, tugging it around her body and doing up the buttons with suspicious haste. But Cally's indignation faded beneath the blatant hunger in his eyes when they met hers. Her flush deepened and her gaze skittered away from his.

"Coffee?" She nodded, rising up on her knees to accept the mug he handed her. She took a quick sip, hoping that her sudden attack of shyness wasn't too obvious. She darted a quick look at him and then looked away again, hiding her face in the mug. It was absurd, but she was intensely aware of the fact that they were sharing the same mug. Ridiculous, considering what they had shared only a few hours ago. She swallowed the warm coffee, trying to banish the foolish uncertainties. Trying to look nonchalant, she reached up to tug her hair from beneath the collar of her shirt.

"Let me."

Cally almost forgot how to breathe as Ryder reached across the short distance between them, brushing aside her hand. He slid his fingers along the back of her neck, lifting the long blond strands from beneath the worn cotton, letting them spill down her back. Cally's fingers tightened around the mug until the sturdy aluminum was in danger of caving in. His hands lingered against the nape of her neck. Slowly, she tilted her head back, letting her eyes meet his. Her free hand came up to rest on his bare chest as he leaned forward. She felt as if she could drown in the deep blue of his eyes. His mustache brushed against her upper lip in the instant before his mouth touched hers.

It was a long slow kiss, full of promise but not demands. Cally sank into it, letting her tongue tangle with his. He tasted of coffee. Or was that her? No matter. All that mattered was that they shared a languid hunger that seemed in keeping with the hot daylight that lay outside.

Ryder drew away first. His eyes met hers for a moment but it was beyond Cally to read any emotion there. Her own emotions were such a tangle of hopes and fears that she couldn't try to guess what he was thinking or feeling.

Ryder had to drag his hands from the spun silk

of her hair. Looking into her eyes, he almost forgot the urgency of his job; the pressing need to get to the village. Her eyes were filled with such a combination of innocence and desire, uncertainty and need. He looked away, afraid of what he might see if he looked deeper.

"I want to get started as soon as possible. We've got a long day ahead of us."

A short time later, they left the small cavern and started down river. Cally cast a few glances over her shoulder at the cave before the jungle swallowed them and blocked off their backtrail. So much had happened there. Her life had been changed forever. It seemed odd to think that she would never see this place again.

She shook off the vague feeling of regret and focused her attention on Ryder's back. She'd left nothing important behind. Everything that mattered lay ahead of her.

CHAPTER ELEVEN

They arrived at the village shortly before dark. Cally thought nothing had ever looked quite so wonderful in her life as did the crude huts and dirt paths of the little community.

The past two hours of walking had been done on pure willpower. Ryder had kept the pace mercilessly steady, not even stopping for lunch. Cally would have protested but she sensed his urgency and kept her arguments to herself. If she was wearing out, she knew that he must be exhausted. Whether he wanted to admit it or not, the fever had taken a lot out of him.

Their arrival caused quite a stir. The quiet of the village was broken by shouts as their presence was noted. Families came to the doors of their huts, watching silently as the two strangers walked tiredly up the dusty incline. Cally swallowed nervously and moved a little closer to Ryder.

"Did they ever have headhunters in Central America?"

Ryder's mouth turned up in a twisted smile.

"They're just curious. They don't see many strangers."

There was a sudden bustle ahead of them and Ryder stopped, his fingers coming out to catch her shoulder, drawing her to a halt. He swayed slightly and she moved closer, silently offering him the support he needed. His fingers tightened for a moment but whether in resentment or gratitude, she couldn't guess.

Ahead, a knot of men was approaching and Cally had to clench her fist to keep from reaching for the reassuring solidity of the gun tucked in her waistband. Ryder didn't seem in the least concerned so she tried to follow his example. The group gradually sorted itself into four people. Three men whose skin was the same dusty brown as the huts around them and a fourth whose shock of gleaming white hair stood out like a beacon in the deepening dusk.

"Hello. You two look as if you're a long way from home."

The voice was smooth as molasses, cultured and made distinctive by an unmistakable French accent. Cally blinked, wondering if she'd actually passed out somewhere in the jungle and was now delirious. This man should have been pouring tea at Versailles, not standing in the middle of a dusty village in Central America. Tall, thin, and angular, his aristocratic features belonged in a gilded frame hanging on the wall of some elaborate château.

"We're a very long way from home, Father." Ryder's voice was husky with exhaustion. Father?

Only then did Cally notice the white collar that circled the neck of the man's worn shirt. "Is there somewhere that my wife and I could rest?"

His fingers tightened on Cally's shoulder, cautioning her to silence but the warning was unnecessary. Cally couldn't have spoken if her life depended on it. Wife?

The priest's eyes skimmed over the two of them, Ryder's dark bulk contrasting with the fragile slenderness of Cally. Even in the gathering darkness, it was easy to see the gray tint beneath Ryder's tan and the exhaustion in Cally's face.

"But of course. You may stay in my home." He turned and murmured a few words to the men who had gathered silently to watch the exchange and two of them moved forward to relieve Ryder of the weight of his pack. He hesitated a moment and then shrugged the straps off his shoulders.

"Why did you lie to him?" Cally asked the question quietly, trying to keep her voice as emotionless as Ryder seemed to be.

He stood across the room from her, looking out a small window at the jungle that loomed so close. They'd both showered in the primitive but effective facilities that Father Duvall's house offered. A kerosene lantern illuminated the room, gilding the simple furnishings. Cally sat cross-legged in the middle of the bed, one of Father Duvall's shirts serving as a nightgown. Ryder wore only the thin towel that he'd brought from the bathroom. All their clothes had been turned over to the villagers to be washed.

Ryder's hand lifted and he took a deep draw on the cigarette he held. He'd shaved and he looked unfamiliar in the small room. Not so piratical but, paradoxically, more dangerous. Smooth and dangerous. His bare shoulders lifted in a shrug.

"I needed an explanation for your presence. Saying that we were married seemed as good as any."

"But why did you have to explain my presence? Why not just tell Father Duvall the truth? It's obvious that he's on our side. He told us that Tomás had been here."

Ryder drew deeply on the cigarette before turning to crush it out in the small ashtray that sat next to the lamp. "It seemed the thing to do at the time."

He looked at her, his eyes darkening as he took in the inviting picture she made. The white shirt wrapped her in virginal color, reminding him that, only a short time ago, the color would have been appropriate. He reached for another cigarette, muttering a curse when the match didn't light until the second try.

"But why didn't you tell him the truth later? I mean, it's pretty obvious that he would help us whether we were married or not. He probably suspects something. I'm not wearing a wedding ring, after all."

Her persistence grated on his nerves, making him look too closely at his motives, making him look at things he didn't want to see.

"What's the big deal?"

Cally lowered her eyes so that she didn't see the

tension in his face. "It's no big deal, I guess. It just seems a little odd." She shrugged. "I suppose I feel bad about lying to Father Duvall. He's been so nice and besides, he's a priest. It doesn't seem quite right. I—"

"Dammit!" Ryder ground the half-smoked cigarette into the ashtray, hardly aware of the way she jumped at his harsh exclamation. "If it bothers you so damn much, I'll go get him out of bed and confess. Will that make you drop it?"

Cally was so stunned by his sudden explosion that he was almost to the door before she gathered her wits and scrambled off the bed. She caught his hand before he could open the door, leaning back against the panel and looking up at him, eyes wide and confused.

"I'm sorry, Ryder. I didn't mean to upset you. It just seemed odd. I . . ."

"Shut up." He enforced the order by the simple method of covering her mouth with his. Cally was frozen for a moment, unable to figure out how they'd gotten from a rational discussion to this. One of his hands came to rest on the door next to her head, the other came up to wrap itself in the shining fall of hair that spilled over her shoulders. When his head lifted, Cally could only gape at him. Her palms were resting on his bare chest but she had no memory of putting them there.

"I told him that we were married because I couldn't stand the thought of not having you in my bed." The words rasped out as his hand left her hair to work the buttons on the shirt. "Is that what you wanted to know?"

Cally shook her head. "I didn't mean . . ." The words trailed off as his palm cupped her breast, lifting it free of the loosened shirt. "Ryder." Her hands lifted to his shoulders, clinging dazedly as his hands slid around her back, pulling her forward until her breasts were pressed against his chest. His mouth caught hers in a long, drugging kiss, leaving her breathless.

"Ryder, I . . ." He kissed her again, sending her thoughts scattering.

"You talk too much." He bent and lifted her easily in his arms, carrying her to the bed where Cally forgot everything but the pleasure of his hands.

From that night on, Cally promised herself that she would not ask questions. At least not for a while. For now, she would just accept whatever the gods felt like giving her. In this time, in this place, she was Ryder's wife. That was all she was going to think about.

The village was small but Father Duvall's efforts had made it unusually prosperous. Scrubby fields provided a living from the thin jungle soil. The women of the village wove exquisite cloth that was exported to the United States. The men fished and hunted. Life was hard by the standards of the modern world but, for the moment, everyone was fed and there was no serious illness in the village. Life could certainly be much worse.

If she had stopped to think about it, Cally might have been amazed at how happy she was. After all, she was hardly out of danger yet; she still didn't know if her uncle was well; she was far from family and friends and she had no one that she could rely on except Ryder. And he was enigmatic and uncommunicative.

Logically, she should have been worried and anxious to get back to civilization. But logic had nothing to do with her emotions. This space in time was an island in the midst of a storm. When they left here, the real world would close in on them and she knew that the pressures in that world might be enough to tear apart the fragile relationship she and Ryder had built. She was going to savor every moment she could in the here and now and let the future take care of itself.

She divided her time between weaving lessons with the village women and just spending time with Ryder.

With each day that passed, she found herself becoming more sure of her feelings for him. It didn't matter that she knew nothing about his past. It didn't matter that he was resisting every deepening step of their relationship. She'd seen through the hard exterior to the gentleness inside and she'd fallen in love with both sides of him.

For Ryder's part, he avoided putting a label on what he was feeling. Cally brought a light into his life like nothing he'd ever known before. She made him smile. She made him remember a different time, before he'd grown to feel so old and hard.

He wiped his greasy hands on a rag, his eyes thoughtful as he watched Cally walk down the dusty street that constituted the only road into or out of the village. In her own jeans and a shirt of his, she looked alluringly feminine. His eyes narrowed, remembering the way her body felt beneath his, the smoky passion in her eyes when he held her.

"She is a very beautiful young woman." Ryder jerked his eyes away from Cally to meet Father Duvall's wise gaze. It was disconcerting to feel a flush climb his throat. He was long past the blushing age.

"Yes, she is." He turned his attention back to the engine compartment of the ancient jeep he was trying to put back in running order. "This jeep is practically a collector's item. I don't know how it's run as long as it has."

"God provides. He kept it running until you arrived and offered your skills."

"It's little enough to do in exchange for your hospitality, Father."

"Just having you and your lovely wife here is repayment enough. I don't often have such stimulating company. And that you both speak French is an added bonus. To hear my mother tongue."

"Even if Cally's accent does make you wince?" Ryder's voice was threaded with amusement and the old priest laughed softly.

"She makes up for the accent with her willingness to try new things. She is a very special woman, and you make a charming couple."

"Thank you." Ryder tugged at a spark-plug wire, testing it for rot. He didn't like the feeling of guilt that seeped into him whenever he thought about lying to Father Duvall.

"It's too bad you aren't really married."

Ryder's head connected with the hood of the jeep and the exclamation that escaped him was one he'd never intended to utter in the priest's presence. He spun around, meeting Father Duvall's gaze and the denial died unspoken. He'd never been of a religious nature but there was something about the man that made it impossible to look him in the eye and lie to him.

"How long have you known?" he asked with resignation.

"Almost from the first moment. Neither of you wears a wedding ring but it isn't really that." The old man tugged on his lower lip, his expression thoughtful. "You lack that certain air that married couples have. There's still too much uncertainty in your relationship."

"It seemed the best thing to do at the time." The excuse sounded even more lame now than it had when he'd tried it on Cally.

"I'm sure you had your reasons. But take my advice and make the lie a truth. It would be a foolish man who'd let her get away."

As if on cue, Cally stepped out of a hut at the other end of the village and waved at him, gesturing toward the river to indicate that she was going to go help with the laundry ritual. Ryder lifted his hand in acknowledgment, his eyes following her as she left with a group of village women. Her hair caught the sunlight in a gleaming braid of silver blond, a vivid contrast to the women around her. Her laugh floated back on a breeze, young and happy.

"A very foolish man." Ryder dragged his gaze back to Father Duvall.

"She's too young." The words came out without conscious thought.

"Too young to marry but not too young to take to your bed?" The priest's aristocratic brows rose in silent comment.

"Father, you've spent a lot of time here. In the rest of the world, marriage does not have quite the value that it once did."

"I've spent a great deal more time in the real world than you have and I know as much about the needs and desires of the flesh as you do. A man does not cease to be a man because he dons a priest's robes. And, even if he did, we are told much in the confessional. I know that the way you watch that woman has more to do with emotional needs than physical. And I've seen the way she watches you."

Ryder's eyes dropped to the wrench in his hand. He felt young and confused. "I've spent a lot of years at the business of war, in one form or another. Half my life. If I was ever as young as she is, it was in another world. How could she possibly understand the things I've done, the things I've been. She is so young. So fresh." His voice died away and he heard the echo of his words in the dusty heat.

The priest said nothing for a long moment and when he spoke, his words were measured. "Some people are born with a certain insight and maturity that age only polishes. Don't throw away happiness by judging someone on years, rather than maturity."

Ryder shook his head, afraid to even contemplate the possible truth in what the other man was saying. "I've seen and done too much."

Father Duvall snorted. "Martyrs are likable only long after they've died, Mr. Allen. Don't hurt Cally and tell yourself that it's for her own good."

In his worn linen shirt and baggy pants, with his thick white hair, the priest was a surprisingly imposing figure and Ryder was reminded of times when he'd been called on the carpet by his own father.

"I—"

Father Duvall interrupted ruthlessly. "And have you given consideration to the possibility of a child? What will you do then? I don't expect an answer from you. It is, after all, none of my business. But you might think about what I've said."

He got up and stalked away before Ryder could summon any reply. Ryder watched him leave, fingers clenched around the wrench he held. He didn't want to hear the truth in what the priest had said. He'd made his choices a long time ago. He'd always known that he would walk alone. Then Cally had come into his life and thrown all his plans out the window. He was drawn to the light she brought into his life, even while he was afraid it would destroy them both.

He turned back to the jeep, muttering under his breath about people who meddled in things that didn't concern them.

The sound of a vehicle roaring up the rough road to the village was so startling that, at first, Cally couldn't even identify the source of the noise. They'd been in the village a week and, in that time, the loudest noise she'd heard had been a child crying.

She cocked her head, finally pinning the growing roar to an engine. Had Ryder finally succeeded in repairing Father Duvall's jeep? But this noise was coming from a distance. The roar intensified and she moved to a window, lifting the coarse curtain slightly until she could look out onto the village street. What if it was Tomás come looking for her and Ryder? She didn't even know where Ryder was.

A battered jeep careened around a corner and slowed as it reached the first of the huts. Edging along the street, the vehicle quickly gathered a crowd of villagers and she could hear shouts of greeting being exchanged. Obviously not Tomás. Whoever this was, the villagers were happy to see them.

She dropped the curtain and opened the door of the house. Perhaps this was the mysterious "contact" that Ryder had been waiting for. The thought brought a confusing mix of emotions that she shoved aside. Ryder strode around the corner of the house and Cally moved toward him but he didn't seem to notice her. The villagers parted as the jeep's occupant stepped out.

"Sara!" Ryder's face broke into the smile Cally had seen all too rarely.

"Ryder! I was beginning to think you'd been eaten by a jaguar."

"No such luck." Sara threw her arms around Ryder and planted a smacking kiss on his mouth and Cally told herself that the shiver that ran up her spine had nothing at all to do with jealousy. *But did he have to respond quite so enthusiastically?*

"How long have you been here?" Sara's voice was soft and husky. Seductive, Cally thought irritably.

"We got here about a week ago."

"We? Who've you got with you?"

Ryder turned, his eyes finding Cally instantly. Cally was somewhat mollified by the way he reached out to grasp her hand and draw her forward. She liked the proprietary message the gesture projected.

"Sara James, meet Cally Stevens."

"Stevens? Wellington's niece?" Sara's laugh was as earthy as her voice and Cally felt her spirits sink. Sara James was tall and buxom, with lively brown eyes and reddish brown hair cut into a short cap of curls that framed her features to best advantage. Beside her, Cally felt pale and wasted. Too young, too boring, too small. From the way they'd greeted each other, it was obvious that Ryder and Sara were old friends and, as far as Cally was concerned, the euphemism could be read as old lovers. Her smile was as pale as she felt.

"Yes. Richard Wellington is my uncle. Do you have any news of him?"

"Only that he won't talk to anyone from the State Department. We weren't even sure that you were missing. All we had were rumors, but Wellington locked himself away in that hospital room and insisted that he could see no one."

"Uncle Richard tends to like to do things his own way."

"That's his reputation. I'm glad to see you're all right, Cally."

I'll just bet you are. Cally smiled and moved a little closer to Ryder, trying to draw comfort from the fact that his arm looped around her shoulders.

By the time they went to bed, Cally's nerves had stretched very close to breaking point. Sara James was charming and witty and she'd entertained Father Duvall and Ryder with her rather wicked imitations of the people she worked with. Cally had smiled in all the right places, laughing when the others did but it was like watching someone else pretend to be her, playing her part while the real Cally shivered inside.

If this was the kind of woman Ryder usually had affairs with, what chance did she stand of turning their affair into something deeper? Sara was a fascinating woman. A woman of the world in a way that could only be gained with age and experience. She was closer to Ryder's age and she lived in his world. She could really understand what his job was like, the pressures that went along with it.

And Ryder was relaxed with Sara, laughing and joking in a way that Cally had never seen before. That they shared a past history together was obvious. There was a feeling of easy intimacy that went deeper than a casual acquaintance.

She'd lost. Before she'd even begun to fight, she'd lost. This, more than anything, showed her how ridiculous it was to think that Ryder could ever want more from her than a simple affair. That she wanted something more was her own problem.

"Sara is going to head back tomorrow and make arrangements to get us to the capital."

"Great." Cally was aware that her response lacked enthusiasm but she couldn't summon up any excitement. It wasn't that she wasn't looking forward to getting back to civilization. The thought of a real bathroom with hot and cold running water and an endless supply of fluffy towels sent shivers of anticipation up her spine. But she had no doubt that when she gained the luxuries of civilized living, she was also going to give up Ryder.

"She'll also find out about your uncle."

"That'll be nice." She kept her back to him and tried not to think about the possibilities of endless nights alone. "You and Sara are obviously old friends."

In the cracked mirror, she saw him shrug. "We've worked together a time or two."

"She seems very nice." The words almost choked her, even though they were true. Under other circumstances, she might have liked Sara.

"I don't know that I'd apply the word nice to her. That seems a little anemic." His mouth curved in a smile that made Cally long to hit him with something very large and very hard. "She's good at what she does."

"I'm sure she is."

He stood up, stretching. Cally watched his reflection, noting the way her pulse picked up and resenting it. She didn't want to want him as much as she did. Not tonight. Tonight she wanted to hate him. She wanted to remember how little she knew about him, not how well her body knew his.

"Ready for bed?"

"You go ahead. I want to stay up for a while."

Her hand froze when she felt his mouth against the nape of her neck.

"Come to bed."

"I'm not tired," she muttered.

"I'm not either."

She stood up abruptly, throwing her hair back and moving away from him. "No. I'm going to read a book."

"Everything Father Duvall has is in French and you don't read French." His bare feet made no sound on the wood floors as he came toward her. Cally moved away just when he would have reached for her. If he touched her, she'd forget everything but the need to feel him a part of her. She had to start ending this now so that the final blow would not be so devastating.

"Maybe I should start learning to read French." She moved around the end of the bed, feeling as if she were being stalked when Ryder moved after her.

"I'll teach you. Later. Right now I have other things in mind."

His hands closed over her shoulders, turning her toward him. Cally kept her eyes down. "I have a headache." The excuse sounded lame even to her own ears.

"Do you? Let me make it go away." She closed her eyes as his mouth brushed across her forehead. It was impossible to ignore him. He was everywhere. If she opened her eyes, it was to see his wide chest only inches away. Behind her lay the bed. In a minute, she knew she would be the one begging him to join her there. The realization of how foolish her dreams were was too painful. She couldn't bear to have him make love to her now. What if he thought of Sara while he was making love to her? The thought was enough to stiffen her weakening resolve.

She pulled away from him suddenly. "Not right now! I'm not in the mood."

She crossed the small room, wishing there were somewhere else to go, wishing that she were wearing something more concealing than just a linen shirt that barely covered her thighs. She could feel his eyes following her but she refused to turn.

"What's wrong? Are you upset about something?"

He sounded so concerned, as if he cared about her. He probably did care. After all, Father Duvall thought they were married. Ryder could hardly go to Sara's bed while they were in the priest's house. If he wanted someone to warm his bed tonight, it would have to be Cally.

"Upset? I'm not upset about anything. I just don't like being used as a substitute." She bit her lip as soon as the words were out. She hadn't planned on saying that. She'd planned on being very adult about the whole thing.

"A substitute? For what?"

She turned to look at him, feeling her anger flare at the look of confusion in his eyes. "Don't you mean 'for whom'?"

His brow rose and Cally wanted to hit him. "I saw the way you were looking at her. It's none of my business but I'm not going to let you make love to me when it's really Sara who you want." She spun away, furious with herself for revealing her feelings. Now he'd know that she was jealous.

In the mirror, she saw him reach for his cigarettes and light one, his eyes on her back. He exhaled a cloud of smoke and studied her rigid spine a moment longer before speaking.

"You're way off base."

"I suppose you're going to tell me that the two of you haven't been lovers? I'm not that stupid. I saw the way you looked at each other."

"What Sara and I have been to each other has

nothing to do with you. If I wanted Sara, what would I be doing in here?"

"Father Duvall thinks we're married. He'd never stand for you going to Sara."

His brow formed a black question mark on his forehead. "If I really wanted to sleep with Sara, do you really think Father Duvall's opinion would stop me? Besides, he knows we aren't married."

He dropped the bomb casually, his eyes amused as Cally spun to face him.

"He knows? Since when?"

Ryder shrugged. "Apparently since the first. He told me two days ago that he knew we weren't married."

"Why didn't you say something to me?"

"What difference would it have made?"

"Well, I wouldn't have . . . I mean we wouldn't have . . ."

"You'd have moved out of this room."

"Well, yes. He's a priest, for heaven's sake."

"That's why I didn't tell you." He stubbed out his cigarette and crossed the room until he stood just in front of her. Cally's nostrils flared nervously, taking in the mingled scents of smoke and some indefinable odor that belonged only to him. His hands came up to slide beneath the weight of her hair, tilting her head back until her eyes met his.

"I told him we were married because I wanted you in my bed. Nothing's changed about that. I don't care what Father Duvall thinks. I'm here because I want you so badly that I live through the days imagining what the nights are going to be like."

Cally couldn't drag her eyes away from the smoldering blue of his. His voice had dropped to a husky whisper that was as arousing as a physical caress. She could feel her body leaning toward him, the heat rising inside.

"Ryder." She wasn't sure what she was asking for. She wanted him to let her go so that she could gather her defenses together. She wanted him to pull her closer, to drown out her doubts with his body.

"I want you. I don't want Sara. I want only you."

Her hands lifted to his chest, her fingers sinking into the dark curls. She could feel herself leaning toward him, wanting him. Would it do so much harm to take this one more night? If what he said was true, then perhaps there was some hope for her dreams after all. And, even if everything would end between them when they left this village, would one more night do any harm? She wouldn't hurt any more when the time came to end it.

"Are you sure?"

"Can't you feel how much I want you?" He pulled her closer, letting her feel the strength of his need.

"Oh, Ryder, I have a feeling I'm going to end up hurt."

His mustache brushed across her forehead. "I don't want to hurt you."

Her mouth shook as she smiled up at him, meeting the blue of his eyes. "Make love to me. I don't want to think about anything but you."

When his mouth found hers, she forced herself to smother all her doubts and fears and think only of the moment.

CHAPTER TWELVE

"Shouldn't take more than four, maybe five, days to make arrangements. You two are precious cargo and we want to be sure you get to the capital safely." Sara polished off the last of her breakfast as she spoke.

Cally glanced at Ryder but he didn't even seem to be aware that there was a conversation going on so she picked up the slack. "How will we be traveling?"

"By jeep at first. Not the most comfortable method but the only one that's practical. It'll take a couple of days by jeep and then we'll pick up a plane and make the hop to the coast. There are a lot of people waiting in the capital who are eager to talk to both of you."

She poured herself another cup of coffee and Cally stole another look at Ryder. He'd been so quiet this morning. Not that he had ever been the outgoing type, but he'd barely said two words since waking.

Sara pushed back her chair. "Well, I'll get started. Expect me by the end of the week."

"Wait a minute." Cally jumped when Ryder spoke. She looked at him, wondering what had put that edge of urgency in his voice. Last night's passionate lovemaking hadn't totally stilled her anxiety about Sara and she didn't want to see anything delay the woman's departure.

Ryder glanced at Cally, and then looked across the table to where Father Duvall sat. Cally watched him, wondering at the tension in his face.

"I'd like for you to marry us, Father. Sara can be a witness."

The silence at the table was so thick, it could almost be seen. In some distant part of her mind, Cally inventoried the expressions on her companions' faces. Father Duvall looked surprised and then pleased, his thin face settling into a gentle smile. Sara's vibrant features went through several rapid changes. Shock, regret and then acceptance —all flitted through her eyes. Ryder's expression remained impassive, unreadable. He might have just asked someone to pass the salt.

Cally could only guess at what her own face must be revealing. She felt as if someone had just kicked her in the diaphragm, pushing out all the air and leaving her gasping. She pushed back her chair and stood up, willing her shaking knees to support her.

Ryder caught up with her outside the door of the bedroom they'd been sharing. She felt his hand close over her shoulder and she stopped, allowing him to turn her toward him but refusing to lift her eyes to his face.

216

"Cally? What's the matter?"

How could he ask?

"I thought you'd be pleased."

He had to be kidding.

"Cally?"

"If you don't let go of me, I'm going to do my best to remove your gizzard through your ear." She got the words out between clenched teeth, addressing his collarbone because she was afraid that if she looked at his face, she would either break down and howl like a baby or she'd punch him. Startled by her venom, Ryder's hands dropped away from her and she spun away and stalked into the bedroom, shutting the door behind her. It didn't keep him out for long. She heard the door open and shut but she refused to turn around.

"You're angry." The statement held a note of surprise and she ground her teeth together, wondering how such an intelligent man could be so stupid.

"Angry? That doesn't begin to describe it."

"I thought you'd want to get married."

She spun around, meeting the confusion in his eyes with a turmoil of emotion in hers. "That has nothing to do with it!"

"Then why are you angry?"

"Did it ever occur to you to ask me what I wanted? Did you consider that I might not like you just taking my answer for granted?"

Ryder glanced away from the smoky gray of her eyes. It had occurred to him. He hadn't wanted to give her a chance to say no.

"Don't you want to marry me?"

"That's not the point! A person likes to be asked about something like that, not have it announced over the breakfast table."

She turned away, blinking back tears of anger and confusion. How could he be so obtuse? She felt him come up behind her a moment before his hands closed around her upper arms, drawing her back against him. She held herself stiff, refusing to lean on his strength.

"Will you marry me?" His voice was husky, threatening to melt the stiffness from her.

"It would be crazy." She had to force the statement out past the little voice that wanted to shout yes without questioning.

"No, it wouldn't. Look how well we've managed to get along together. Marry me." His mouth touched the delicate skin on the back of her neck, setting off shivers of awareness.

"We haven't known each other very long." The protest was weak. She *wanted* to marry him. There was nothing in the world she wanted more except perhaps to have him say that he loved her.

"We've known each other long enough. Marry me, Cally."

If he wanted her to marry him, didn't that indicate that he cared for her? Maybe he couldn't say the words yet but didn't actions always speak louder than words anyway?

"I don't know . . ."

"I do. Marry me." He pulled her closer, letting her feel the heat of him against her back. Would it be so awful to take the chance? They'd gone through so much together. If they could manage under the conditions they'd faced so far, wouldn't normal life be a piece of cake?

There were gaps in her reasoning. Cally knew that as well as anyone but she didn't want to look at the gaps. It could work. She'd make it work. She closed her eyes, shutting out the faint voice of reason that insisted this was crazy.

"Yes. I'll marry you."

She had no cause to regret her decision in the days that followed. The ceremony had been so brief that it might have been possible to believe it had all been a dream, except for the immediate difference it made in Ryder. It was as if, when he slipped the ring on her finger, he slipped out from under a thousand cares.

Cally studied the narrow gold band on her left hand, wondering if there was some magic in it that had changed Ryder from the rather taciturn man she'd fallen in love with to this younger, happier, more enthralling person. She was discovering a playful side of him that she'd never known existed. In the few days since they'd married, he'd laughed more than in all the time she'd known him. Of course, there'd been little to laugh about since she'd been thrown into his life. Maybe this happy person was the real Ryder Allen.

Four to five days, Sara had said. They'd have that much time together as husband and wife before they had to face the rest of the world. Cally was determined to make the most of every minute and Ryder seemed to share her feelings.

"Pass me that wrench, would you?" His voice echoed out of the engine compartment of the jeep.

"Did you just ask me to pass you a wench?" Cally picked up the tool he'd requested and held it up as he pulled his head out from under the hood.

Ryder took in the picture she made, sitting in the thin shade beside the jeep. Her jeans had seen one adventure too many and she'd cut the tattered legs off to make a pair of shorts. Her legs were stretched out of the shade, catching the late-afternoon sunshine that streamed down on the quiet village. She still wore one of his shirts but she'd tied the long tails into a knot under her breasts, exposing a thin band of midriff.

She looked as if she hadn't a care in the world. Her eyes met his mock scowl with a hint of mischief in their depths. She held up the wrench with an apologetic shrug.

"Well, it sounded like you said wench."

He took the wrench from her and set it down on the fender before picking up a greasy rag to wipe his hands on. "The only wench around here is you. And an impertinent one you are at that."

She batted her lashes at him. "I'm sorry."

"No, you're not." He set down the rag and stepped forward, his eyes gleaming with intent. Cally cowered back against the jeep, trying to look properly terrified. "Impertinent wenches need to be disciplined before they get out of hand."

"Oh, please, kind sir. I'm sorry I offended you."

She spoiled the apology by giggling. Father Duvall was gone for the day, having left at dawn to walk to another village. They had the house to themselves and Cally had the feeling that they were about to make the most of their privacy.

"If you're truly sorry, wench, you'll have to prove it to me. My temper is hot and it will take much to cool it."

"Oh please sir. I'm really, truly sorry." She reached behind her. It was difficult to think with him looming over her but she was enjoying the game. Her fingers closed around the glass of water she'd been sipping on for the past hour. "I think I can cool your hot temper."

She stood up, keeping her right hand behind her, hoping he wouldn't be suspicious.

"It will take a lot," he warned her.

"I think this might do it." The water caught him squarely in the face and Cally caught only a glimpse of his stunned expression before she spun on one bare foot and ran for the house, proving that she was not only an impertinent wench but a cowardly one as well.

She sprinted up the stairs and flung open the door, rushing into the dim interior of the house. Her heart was pounding with excitement. Had she gone too far?

He caught her in the bedroom doorway, his arm catching her around the waist and spinning her into the hard muscles of his chest. Cally's shriek was only half in fun. Ryder's anger could be formidable. What if he was truly angry with her?

Crushed against his chest, her hands trapped between them, she raised her eyes to his face. Relief swept through her when she saw the gleam in his eyes.

"Your punishment will be much worse now, my pretty."

His head dipped and her mouth softened in anticipation of his kiss. It caught her totally off guard when he shook his head, shaking water off his damp hair into her face.

"Beast!"

"Revenge is sweet."

She pushed at his chest but he refused to allow her to free her hands. "Let me wipe my face, brute."

His expression took on sanctimonious overtones as he looked down at her. "It's not nice to call names."

"It's not nice to get a person all wet and then not let them dry their face."

"Poor baby. Let me help you." He bent and began to kiss the droplets from her face, his mouth lingering against her skin, letting her feel the brush of his mustache. Cally went limp against him.

Ryder's mouth explored the delicate line of her jaw, pausing to nip at the lobe of her ear before creeping toward her mouth. "I told you that impertinent wenches had to be punished."

"I'll have to remember to be impertinent more often." His mouth closed over hers as he lifted her in his arms and carried her toward the bed.

It was quite a while before he got back to work on the jeep.

Much as she savored this newfound playfulness in him, she found herself becoming more aware of how little she knew about the man she'd married. She knew nothing of his past and, as a student of history, she was a firm believer in knowing the past to understand the present. To understand the man he was, she needed to know something of how he'd come to be where he was.

Lying in bed, bright moonlight streaming in through the open curtains, she was aware that their time alone was running out. Tomorrow would be five days. If Sara's estimate was accurate, they could be leaving the village tomorrow. They'd have company on the trip to the capital and, once there, there'd be questions to answer and people to see. Things that would intrude into the fragile shell of intimacy they'd built. This might be the last chance she'd have to really talk to Ryder for a long time.

He lay on his side next to her, his hand idly sifting through her hair. He seemed fascinated by the feel of her hair, wrapping his hands in it as they made love, drawing it around her body to form a silky veil.

They'd made love less than an hour ago and she wondered if it was her imagination that had put an edge of desperation in his touch. Was he also aware of their limited time alone? She wanted to lie here and just savor the closeness but she needed to know something of the man she'd married.

"Who was Joe?"

Ryder stiffened, his fingers stilling in her hair. There was a moment of silence and then he rolled away and sat up. He sat up on the edge of the bed, reaching for his cigarettes.

"Why do you ask?" The sharp scent of sulfur caught in her nostrils as he struck a match.

She sat up, pulling the sheet over her breasts, tucking her legs under her. Even in the moonlight, she could see the tension that tightened the muscles in his back.

"You talked about him when you were feverish."

"Did I?" The glowing tip of the cigarette marked the motion of his hand as he brought it to his mouth. It was obvious that he didn't want to talk about it and Cally was tempted to just drop the whole subject but something told her that she might have found a key to at least partially unravel some of the many mysteries that surrounded him.

"You called his name and asked him not to die." His shoulders twitched as if she'd placed a strap across them. "Who was he, Ryder?"

The silence stretched out between them and she held her breath, praying that she hadn't made a mistake by bringing it up. But they were married now and, if there was to be any future for them beyond the confines of this village, then Ryder had to open up to her, at least a little bit.

"He was my gunner in 'Nam." He broke the

silence so abruptly that it seemed to shatter like glass. "He was just a kid. Hell, we were all just kids." The cigarette rose and fell again.

"I didn't know that you were in Vietnam."

"Wasn't everybody?" There was bitter humor in the question. He took another puff of the cigarette. "I was a chopper pilot. Joe was my gunner on my last tour."

"What happened?"

He smoked silently for a long time and Cally wondered if he'd even heard her soft question.

"He died." The flat statement echoed in the quiet room, all the more poignant for its lack of drama. "The chopper was hit and I couldn't keep it in the air. We caught a lot of fire going down. I wasn't hurt and I dragged Joe free. He'd been hit. Once. Maybe twice. There was a lot of blood, I couldn't tell exactly where he was hurt. We hid out in the jungle. He never lost consciousness and he kept telling me that he was going to get a Purple Heart and he'd get to go home to recuperate."

He lit another cigarette and then stubbed out the old one, his movements angry. "He was a farmboy from Georgia and he kept talking about how great it was going to be to get home and have fried chicken and biscuits and all the trimmings. His mom would make a big pitcher of lemonade and his little brothers would make ice cream on the back porch. That was all he talked about.

"And all the time, we were waiting to see who'd find us first—our side or theirs."

225

Cally stared at his taut back, trying to think of something to say, some comfort she could offer.

"I couldn't get the bleeding to stop. I knew he was dying. I don't know if he knew it too. We finally heard a chopper and we knew we were going to be lifted out. I remember reaching for him and he grabbed my arm and looked at me so intently and he told me that he wanted me to go home to Georgia with him. He said his mom would like me."

Cally could see that his hands were shaking. She sniffed quietly, wiping her eyes with the back of her hand.

"The chopper set down in a rice field and I picked him up and ran. There was gunfire from the jungle and they were firing cover for us from the chopper. I didn't even know I'd been hit until we were in the air. Took a bullet in the leg. I got Joe into the chopper and we lifted but he was already dead."

He stared down at his shaking hands for a moment. The silence in the room created a heavy blanket full of emotions. Cally gulped, trying to swallow a sob. She'd wanted to get to know him but she'd never intended to cause him so much pain.

"We each got a Purple Heart and I went home with Joe's body. He had a great family and since I was a friend of Joe's, I was a member of the family, too. I stayed there while my leg healed. Every Sunday afternoon, his mom made fried chicken and all the trimmings." He stopped abruptly and Cally had the feeling that if he had continued, his voice would have broken.

She swallowed, trying to force down the tears that had settled into a lump in her throat. "What about your family? You've never mentioned them."

"What is this? Twenty questions?"

"It's just that I don't really know anything about you. We're married and I don't even know if I have any in-laws."

For a moment, she thought he wasn't going to answer her and then he shrugged and turned so that he faced her. It was impossible to read his expression. The moonlight was too shallow to show more than the planes and angles of his features.

"I have a sister and a brother. I'm the oldest. My parents are alive and they all live in a small town in New England."

"Do you see them very much?"

"Not much." He hesitated. "I was home about eight years ago."

"That's a long time." She was careful to keep her tone neutral. She wasn't passing any judgments.

"A long time." He stubbed out his cigarette, his movements as brisk as his words. "I'm a little too rough around the edges to have much to say to my family anymore. They're good people but none of them have been farther than five hundred miles from the town where we were born. My great-grandparents built the house I was raised in and ten miles down the road is the house that their parents built. It went to the oldest son and my great-grandfather built my parents' home."

"It sounds very nice. I used to wish that my family had a more stable background. I guess we've always been wanderers. I always wanted to be able to point to something and say that it had belonged to my great-grandmother."

"It was nice when I was a kid. And, maybe, if the war hadn't interfered, I would have stayed in New England and had children and never gone farther than five hundred miles from home. But you can't go back. I changed too much in 'Nam. I saw too much. Last time I was home, my mother watched me like I was a stick of dynamite set to explode. And maybe I was."

He closed the subject before Cally could think of anything to say. "It's late. We'd better get to bed. No telling what tomorrow may be like."

Cally slid back under the covers, wondering if it had been wise to question him. She'd gotten answers, many of them much as she had expected. But it hadn't been answers she'd really wanted. It was trust. She wanted him to trust her enough to open up to her. And she still wasn't sure if she had that trust.

Ryder lay down, his body stiff next to hers. Cally hesitated. She didn't have to be an expert in body language to read the message in his rigid position. Maybe it would be best to allow him his distance for now. But, even as she was thinking that, she was reaching across the bed, snuggling against his side, needing his warmth. For a moment longer, he stayed rigid and she was afraid her questions had jeopardized the progress they'd made. With an almost convulsive movement, his arms slid around her, drawing her tight against his side and he buried his face in her hair. It was not a comfortable position—he was holding her too tight —but she didn't care. Whether he would admit it in so many words or not, he needed her.

She put her arms around him, holding him, wishing that she could wipe out the pain he'd suffered, and knowing that all she could do was offer him her love and hope it eased some of the old hurts.

Ryder was up and gone before Cally woke the next morning. She stretched, her hand reaching out for him and finding the bed empty. Her eyes opened on a frown of disappointment. They'd fallen asleep so closely entwined that she felt bereft at finding herself alone.

Before she had a chance to do more than swing her feet out of bed, the door opened and Ryder stepped into the room. She watched him, wondering what she'd see in his eyes. He glanced up from the sheaf of papers he was studying and their eyes met. He looked vaguely wary, as if not quite certain of his reception. Cally smiled, letting her love show without reservation.

He crossed the room quickly and his free hand cupped the back of her head, tilting her face for his kiss. A kiss that was long and passionate.

"Good morning." The greeting was breathless

and she wondered if he could tell that her heart was beating double time.

"Good morning." He brushed his thumb over her mouth, his hand lingering on her face before dropping away. "You'd better get dressed. Sara is back and we're leaving as soon as possible."

The announcement brought such a conflicting tangle of emotions that Cally didn't even try to sort them all out. "Did she have any news about Uncle Richard?"

Ryder's grin reassured her even before his words. "She managed to get in to see your uncle and he made an amazing recovery once he heard that you were safe and sound. He was afraid to bring in the government because they've bungled these kinds of things before but he knew if he gave Tomás what he wanted, you'd never be returned in one piece. So he figured that if he was too sick to get the ransom notes, it might buy you some time."

"Thank heavens." She began to pull on clothes. "What about Tomás?" She shivered, remembering the venom in the stocky man's eyes. "Have they caught him?"

"Not yet. It's going to take a little while. Sara took back the information I got and the government is going to set a trap for him. I think Tomás is in for a big surprise. You and I will have to lie low for a couple of days once we're back in the capital. I want Tomás to continue to think that I cut out only to save your life. If he figures out that I'd been working for our government, he might change plans and that would mean the trap would spring on nothing."

Cally looked around the plain little room. "I'm going to miss this place."

"Come on, you've been dying for a real hot bath for weeks."

"Yeah, but I've grown fond of this place." She looked at him. "I've been happy here."

His face softened. "I have too. For the first time in a very long time."

And as long as she could take the smile in his eyes with her, she didn't mind leaving anything else behind.

She was to pull that smile out more than once in the days that followed. It was just about the last one she saw from him. From the moment they said good-bye to Father Duvall and left the little village behind, Ryder seemed to start drawing back into his old shell.

It might have been that he was back among his own kind. Sara had brought three other agents with her, all male and they all had that same hard-edged air of not caring. They were polite to Cally but it was clear that these were people accustomed to living on the edge in a way that she could only imagine.

The trip to the coast took almost three days and Cally could see Ryder slipping away from her. The only thing that kept her from going completely crazy was the way he kept her close at all times. She was rarely more than an arm's reach away and, at night, she slept tight in his arms, his fingers tangled in her hair as if to bind her to him.

The closer they got to civilization, the more she worried about what was going to happen to the two of them. It seemed like years instead of weeks since she'd been kidnapped. She wasn't even sure she knew how to talk to other people anymore. She certainly didn't have much to say to their traveling companions but then they didn't have much to say to her either.

When they arrived at the small town where they were to catch a plane to take them to the capital, Cally felt almost smothered by the presence of so many people. Ryder seemed to sense her disorientation. His arm slid around her, drawing her closer to him in the confines of the van. She was aware of Sara's eyes on them as Ryder's head bent over hers.

"It's natural to feel like a visitor from another planet. You'll adjust quicker than you think."

She wound her fingers through his, not even caring if her uncertainty was obvious. "I hope so. There are so many people."

He smiled. "It's really a pretty small town. Wait till we get to the capital. That's where you'll really feel the culture shock."

"I can hardly wait."

The flight to the capital was short. Too short, as far as Cally was concerned. Ryder conferred with Sara in a conversation that was too quiet for Cally to hear. Watching him from the corner of her eye, she had the feeling that the closeness she'd felt growing between them had been a dream. This was not the man who'd laughed with her, who'd made love to her as if the world could come to an end tomorrow and it wouldn't matter as long as they were together. This wasn't even the man she'd first met in the guerrilla camp, who'd been kind to her, however reluctantly.

This was someone new. Someone hard and frightening.

She shook the thought away, turning to look out the window as the plane began its descent. What had begun to grow between them had not been her imagination. They'd laid a foundation for a solid relationship and she was going to believe that it was a strong foundation. Things might be rocky for a while—what new marriage wasn't?—but they were going to make it. Together.

CHAPTER THIRTEEN

"I'm not going anywhere without you." Cally's jaw set stubbornly.

"Cally, it doesn't make any sense for you to stay here." Ryder's tone of sweet reason only made her more determined to stay.

"It makes sense to me."

"Cally, I really do think it would be best if you came home with me. Ryder can finish up his business here and then meet us back in LA."

Cally's face softened as she met her uncle's clear gray eyes, so like her own. She knew that he was well aware that his round face made him look like a cherub and he was not above using that fact to his advantage. More than one business rival had been thrown off guard by Richard Wellington's harmless exterior. Still, he *had* been worried and he had spent the last month trapped in a hospital room for her sake. But she wasn't going home to the States with him. Not without Ryder.

"I'm sorry, Uncle Richard. I'm staying with my husband." She used the word deliberately, reminding them both of the exact status of her relationship to Ryder. Her uncle blinked, his gaze shifting to Ryder.

"Husband. I keep forgetting." What he meant was that he *wanted* to forget and Cally didn't entirely blame him for that.

She might be in love but she wasn't blind to what her uncle was seeing. His niece, whom he loved even if he didn't always understand her, had disappeared for over a month. She had returned, alive and well but accompanied by a man whom he was supposed to accept as her husband. A man who didn't fit any profile of nephew-in-law that Richard had ever imagined. Even when he smiled, Ryder looked exactly what he was—a man who'd spent a lot of years living on the edge, a man who'd killed and would kill again if he had to. This was not the fresh-faced college boy her uncle expected her to bring home.

"Look, we're not going to be here that much longer, are we?" She looked up at Ryder and he nodded reluctantly.

"Two, maybe three weeks. We should have Tomás in hand by then."

"See, Uncle Richard, it won't be that long before I'll be home."

"But that extra two or three weeks would give you time to get ready for school in the fall. You haven't even registered yet."

"I'm not going to be going to school this quarter." She continued quickly, trying to forestall the protest she could see exploding out of him. "I need some time to evaluate the direction I've been head-ing in. It's only for the quarter. I'm planning on starting again in January."

"Just because you're married, there's no reason to give up your education, Cally. If money is a problem, you know your aunt and I would be more than happy . . ."

"I'm capable of supporting my wife, Mr. Wellington." There was an edge to Ryder's voice.

"Of course. I didn't think . . ." Cally took pity on her uncle's flustered attempt at apology. Ryder made him nervous and she suspected that her husband knew exactly what he was doing.

"Uncle Richard, I've gone through a lot in the last few weeks. It's only because Ryder was there that I'm alive at all. An experience like that can't help but change a person. I'm not sure my goals are the same anymore. I know I'm not the same person I was a month ago. I'm not giving up on my education. I'm just doing a little reevaluating. You do that in your businesses all the time," she coaxed.

Richard Wellington knew when he was beaten. He stared into Cally's gray eyes, seeing the stubborn determination behind the coaxing. She was going to do what she pleased, with or without his blessing. She'd always been like that. The sweetest, politest child you'd ever want to know but once she was determined about something, you couldn't stop her for love or money. And she looked so much like her mother that he didn't even have the heart to argue with her. His sister had also had the ability to wrap him around her little finger without effort.

He glanced at the man who sat so silently next to her. Well, she'd be safe enough with him. He was reserving judgment on this whole marriage thing but he couldn't deny that it was thanks to this man that his niece was alive.

"Your aunt is going to flay me when I come home without you," he muttered as he rose. Cally stood up and put her arms around him, giving him a hug.

"You and I both know that Aunt Sylvia wouldn't hurt a flea. Just tell her that I dug in my heels and you'll have all her sympathy. You know that she thinks I'm too pigheaded for my own good."

"She's right, too." But there was no heat in the words. Richard Wellington was always gracious in defeat. "I hope the two of you will stay here. I keep this suite for my own use when I'm down here and it's just empty when I'm not around."

"That sounds fine to me. Ryder?"

Ryder glanced around the luxuriously appointed room and contrasted it with the accommodations he'd had for the past few months. He shrugged, his mouth twisting in a tight smile.

"That's very kind of you, Mr. Wellington." If he'd been alone, he'd have refused the offer and found his own accommodations, something where he didn't feel quite so much like a bull in a china shop. But he wasn't alone. He had to remember Cally.

Despite Cally's determination to stay with Ryder, she felt tearful watching her uncle leave. She sniffed as the hotel door shut behind him. In a funny way, it was like leaving home for the last time. If she'd gone with him, she would have been going back to everything that was safe and familiar. Instead, she'd chosen to stay in a country where she'd experienced the most terrifying moments of her life.

"You should have gone with him."

She turned to look at Ryder. He was standing in the middle of the living room, legs apart, balanced on the balls of his feet as if braced for a fight. As usual, his expression was difficult to read but she thought she saw wariness hovering in his eyes.

"I didn't want to go with him. I wanted to stay here with you."

He didn't respond, didn't argue because he wanted her with him as much as she wanted to stay. "How long till you'll have your degree?"

"Three quarters or so."

"Another full school year, then."

"Yes." She watched him cross to the window, trying to identify the undercurrents she was sensing. He was edgy. They were safe in a luxurious hotel room, both of them had been provided with clean clothing, there'd been time for a wonderful hot bath for her, and Ryder had showered and shaved. In a few hours, he would be meeting with the people he worked for to give them a full report.

In short, everything was going their way. The pressure he'd been under for months was off his shoulders. He should be relaxing, unwinding, tasting freedom. Instead, he was as uptight as he'd ever been in Tomás's camp and he might have been another man altogether from the happy bridegroom he'd been after the wedding.

"Does it bother you that I'm still in school?"

His shoulders twitched. "Why should it?"

She moved to stand in front of him. His eyes met hers and he looked less than approachable but Cally refused to be intimidated.

"I think it bothers you that you're thirty-eight and I'm twenty-two. I think you've got the absurd idea that you're too old for me."

"It's not all that absurd," he protested.

"Yes it is. I've never been able to understand why people put so much emphasis on chronological age. What difference does it make how old a person is? What matters is what they're like on the inside."

"That's a very nice view of the world but the facts are that I'm sixteen years older than you. And I've done a lot in those sixteen years. I've done things I'm not proud of; sometimes I've let the end justify the means."

She reached up to put her fingers against his mouth, cutting off his words. "I'm not a fool. I'm not saying that the difference in our ages isn't a factor to be considered. Obviously, we can't just pretend it doesn't exist. All I'm saying is that I don't see why it should be a major issue. It's a fact. That's all."

His free hand came up to catch hers, pulling her

fingers away from his mouth and then keeping hold of them. Cally wondered if he was even consciously aware of the way his thumb stroked over her palm.

"I think you're blinding yourself to the potential problems."

"I'm not seeing problems where they don't exist."

"Your uncle was right. You *are* stubborn and pigheaded." He dropped her hand and he was unprepared for the way she snuggled up against him. His arms circled her automatically.

"We're not going to get anywhere by arguing. I'm willing to let time prove me right."

"You are, are you?" Despite the turmoil he felt inside, he couldn't help but smile when he took in the shameless look in her eyes.

"Certainly. I may be stubborn but I'm also gracious. I promise not to rub your nose in this conversation fifty years from now."

"Fifty years from now, I'll be eighty-eight and probably too deaf to notice if you did rub my nose in it."

"I'll be seventy-two and I'll just shout into your hearing aid." Her fingers worked the buttons on his shirt and he felt desire stir, mixed with despair. She was so young and fresh and beautiful. What could she possibly know about the dark side of life? She opened the last button and slid her palms across the rough surface of his chest.

"Is this how you plan to win all our arguments?" Just for a little while longer, he'd let him-

240

self pretend that it could work. He'd let himself believe that they could have a future.

Her hands slid to his waist, working loose his belt and sliding the zipper of his jeans down. Her eyes were the very picture of innocence as she slipped her hands beneath the stiff fabric to feel the heat of his arousal. Ryder bit his lip to hold back a moan of pure lust.

"Can you think of a better way to win an argument?"

He shook his head, unable to speak for the moment.

"I thought so, too."

His fingers shook as he worked the buttons of her shirt. "You're a shameless hussy."

"I know," she admitted breathlessly. She played with the zipper on his pants. "It's not really your body that I want. It's just that there's a real bed in there and I haven't slept in one in so long." She broke off as his thumb stroked across her nipple.

Ryder's smile was full of satisfaction at the way she melted against him. "So you just want to go take a nap, is that it?"

"Well, I'm not really tired enough to go to sleep. I thought maybe . . ." She broke off, losing her train of thought when he caught her nipple between thumb and forefinger and tugged gently. She closed her eyes as his mustache brushed along the curve of her shoulder, pushing her shirt out of the way as he worked his way to her neck.

"You thought maybe what?" His breath felt hot against her as he nibbled on the taut line of her throat. His fingers continued to torment her breasts.

"I thought maybe we could . . . we could . . . lie on the bed and . . . and talk, maybe. Ryder." His name came out as a low exclamation of surrender. Her hands lifted to his head, her fingers burrowing in his hair, urging the teasing pleasure of his mouth downward.

His hands left her breasts to slide around her hips, lifting her easily until her breasts were on a level with his mouth. "Talk?" He brushed his mustache across the swollen peaks, tormenting her with the promise there. "We could talk if you wanted. What would you like to talk about?"

"Ryder." Her hands tightened in his hair but he ignored their silent pleading.

"Me? I think I'd make a boring subject. What else would you like to talk about?" He flicked his tongue over one swollen nipple. Cally moaned. He was giving her tantalizing hints of what could be. She'd started this game and now she was helpless to end it.

"I don't want to talk." She got the words out between gritted teeth, trying to urge his head closer. He kissed her nipple, brushing across the sensitive surface with his mouth.

"No?" His voice was all innocence, as if he couldn't imagine why she'd changed her mind.

"Ryder, please." She abandoned demand and openly begged him. Her body was on fire. All the heat and flames were held inside, waiting to explode outward as soon as they found an outlet.

"Please what? Please this?" He let her feel the soft roughness of his tongue, drawing another moan from deep inside her. "Or please this?" Cally's fingers burrowed into his hair, her breath leaving her in a low groan as his mouth closed over her at last, drawing on her taut breast with satisfying pressure.

"Yes. Yes." She arched her back, confident in his ability to support her, oblivious to the fact that her toes dangled in midair. All that mattered was the hot pressure of his mouth around her nipple.

He held her there, slaking his thirst at her breasts, driving the flames in both of them to a fever pitch. Outside, the city baked under a hot tropical sun and the hotel's air conditioning worked overtime to keep their guests in cool comfort. But in the luxurious suite on the top floor, the temperature was steamy.

When Ryder at last lowered Cally to her own feet, her knees refused to support her and she had to cling to him. Her hands clutched at his shoulders and she leaned against his chest, feeling the dampness of his skin beneath her flushed face. Her body throbbed with need.

He bent, catching her under the knees and swept her up in his arms. Cally's head fell back on his shoulder and their eyes met. Ryder felt his heart slam against his chest at the mixture of desire and love he read in her eyes. Desire was something he understood but the love was something he was just coming to understand since Cally came into his life. He closed his eyes for a moment, shutting out all thoughts of the future and the difficulties it held. Right here and now, he wanted to pretend that everything was perfect.

Cally could see the conflict in his eyes. She felt his arms tighten around her and saw the mixture of pain and defiance that flickered across his face before he turned to carry her into the bedroom. She wanted to hold him and tell him that everything was going to be all right but she knew he'd never accept that reassurance from her. He believed that there were so many barriers between them. How could she convince him that it didn't have to be that way?

He stopped beside the bed, his eyes still dark and disturbed, and Cally reached up to trace the lines that bracketed his mustache. He'd have to realize for himself that what they had was something special. She couldn't make him accept it.

"Did you plan on standing here all day?" Her voice was husky and inviting and Ryder's eyes darkened in a look that she had no trouble reading. Pure desire. He put one knee on the bed, lowering her slowly onto the mattress, his shoulders blocking out the light as he came down over her.

Despite the urgency that throbbed in the pit of her stomach, she found herself savoring the slow pace he set. Their clothes slid from them, leaving nothing between them except need.

He tasted her need on the skin of her shoulders, in the swollen weight of her breasts, on the taut skin of her belly. Cally twisted restlessly as his mouth skimmed down her leg, pausing to kiss each toe. She drew her knee up, hardly daring to breathe as he kissed his way up the inside of the opposite leg. She felt his breath an instant before she felt his mouth against that most sensitive of places. She arched into his kiss, her breath gusting out. Her fingers clenched in the softness of the bed-spread.

Ryder's hands slid beneath her, cupping her but-tocks, drawing her up into his relentless kiss, driving her toward fulfillment, ignoring her pleading moans as he drew out her pleasure.

Cally felt as if she were caught in a whirlpool, spinning faster and faster as she neared the center. It would have been frightening if Ryder hadn't been the one pushing her forward. The tension building inside made it impossible to think. She could only feel. She was so close. So close.

And suddenly he was gone. The delicious tor-ment of his mouth was gone. Her eyes flickered open to see him above her, his face taut with need. Their eyes met for an instant and then his head lowered, his mouth taking possession of her lips at the same moment that his body took possession of hers.

Cally arched to receive him, her hands running up the damp muscles of his back, searching for something to cling to as the world spun madly around her. He was all there was in the entire world. Above her, within her. There could be nothing in the world beyond this moment; this one instant in time when each took from the other everything they needed. Each giving and taking; fulfilling and being fulfilled.

Ryder groaned as he felt the delicate tremors that shook her body, her fingers digging into his back. He followed her willingly over the edge into the spinning madness, losing himself in her. For this moment, he wouldn't ask for anything more. No future. No past. Only this.

"I'm hungry."

Ryder opened his eyes reluctantly. "You can't be hungry. We just ate."

"That was hours ago and I'm hungry."

"You just want another steak."

"Okay. I admit it. I'm a glutton. If I never see another tortilla, it will be just fine with me. Now, are you going to feed me?"

"No."

"No?" She lifted her head to glare at him indignantly. Since she was sprawled across his chest, her face still flushed with satisfaction, her body glued to his, her indignation fell a bit flat. "You're just going to let me starve?"

He reached up to wind a strand of her hair around his wrist, his face younger, more relaxed than she'd seen it since they left Father Duvall's tiny home. "You don't look like you're in danger of starving."

"Looks can be deceiving," she warned darkly. "If you don't feed me, I'm likely to do something unspeakable to you."

"Sounds interesting." He arched one dark brow and eyed her hopefully.

She laughed, shifting herself to a more comfortable position. "Please, Ryder. I can make you very happy." She twined her fingers in his chest hair, setting her face into vampish lines and settling a little more intimately against his thighs.

He groaned and brought his palm down on her bare bottom. "Behave yourself, hussy. I'm just recovering from the last time you 'made me very happy.' "

She pouted, thrusting out her lower lip in an accurate imitation of a three-year-old. "You're very mean."

"And you love every minute of it. Give me a little time to recover, brat, and I'll see that you get fed." He was enjoying this time with her and he was reluctant to see it end. Soon he had to leave this room and go talk to the men he worked for. The real world would return with a bang and all its assorted problems would come crashing down around them. For just this short time, he didn't want to think about it.

He wrapped her hair around his wrist, contrasting its pale gleam with the heavy tan he'd acquired from too many years in the sun. The contrast seemed apt. Sunshine and night. Gold and teak. The two might meet but they could never combine. No matter how much he might wish otherwise.

He rolled suddenly, taking Cally by surprise as she found herself flat on her back with him looming over her.

"I find I have appetites of a different sort, wench."

"I thought you had to go to a meeting," she got out, breathless beneath the heat of his gaze.

"Let them wait."

If Cally had hoped that the closeness they shared in bed would carry over into the rest of their time together, she was destined for disappointment. Ryder was always a passionate lover but, the rest of the time he was preoccupied.

She cautioned herself to patience, trying to remember that he'd had thirty-eight years to build up the barriers she was trying to knock down. She couldn't expect to succeed overnight.

For Ryder, he looked on the days they spent in the capital as being stolen time. It couldn't last but he was going to enjoy having her with him for now. He'd given up denying to himself that he was in love with her. He didn't know quite how it had happened but, somehow, she'd worked herself into his heart, taking a piece of it for her own.

"Bad news. We made the strike but your friend slipped through our nets." Ryder jerked his attention back to the present.

"What?"

The man who sat across the desk from him winced. John Ryder Allen had a reputation for being a man of great control but rumor had it that you didn't want to see him lose that control. David Harcourt certainly did not want to test that rumor.

"We set up a trap based on the information you

gave us. There was some pretty heavy fighting but we caught them off guard. I think it's safe to say that we've put a major dent in the guerrilla activities against the government. It will take them months to put any workable army back together. You did a terrific job, Allen."

"You said you missed Tomás?" Ryder dismissed the praise without interest.

"He isn't among the prisoners or the dead. We have to assume that he slipped away during the fighting."

"Dammit!" Ryder got to his feet, striding across the room to the dusty window that looked onto an even dustier street. "He'll head straight for the capital. He's got friends here, supporters."

"He could already be here. The fighting started a week ago and there's no way for us to know at what point he slipped away."

Ryder felt a cold shiver work its way down his spine. Somehow, he'd known that he and Tomás weren't finished when he left the guerrilla camp behind. If Tomás found out that he was in the capital, it wouldn't take him long to figure out that Ryder was probably the source of the information that had led to the destruction of his much-vaunted army. Tomás was not the type to forgive and forget.

"If you could give us the names of anyone you know of that he's likely to contact, I can get some men working on it right away. With any luck, we may be able to pick him up before he actually gets to his friends."

"Sure. I'll give you what I can." Ryder rubbed his hand over the back of his neck, trying to dispel the feeling of disaster.

The knock on the door caught Cally in the midst of polishing her fingernails. She muttered a curse, set the brush back in the bottle and carefully wiped at a dab of pale pink polish that was smeared off the nail. She swung her legs off the sofa and crossed to the door, gently waving her fingers in the air.

"Who is it?"

"The maid, señora."

"Drat." Cally carefully grabbed the doorknob with the pads of her fingers, trying not to bump any of the nails. It was eight thirty in the morning, hardly a reasonable hour for maid service but, if she'd learned one thing in the two weeks she'd been here, it was that the hotel staff worked on their own peculiar and erratic timetable. If the maid was here now, she wasn't going to complain. It could be midnight before the woman felt like returning.

She turned away as the door swung open, holding her hands out to admire the effect of the polish on her short nails. It seemed like years since she'd done anything as totally frivolous as polishing her nails.

She heard the maid step into the room and it struck her as odd that the woman didn't say anything. Usually, the maids liked to talk. Cally had learned the life story of every woman who'd cleaned the suite. She started to turn but the movement was never completed. The blow caught her behind the ear. There was an instant of blinding pain and then nothing.

CHAPTER FOURTEEN

"We've located Tomás. He's at a farmhouse less than an hour from the capital."

Ryder stubbed out his cigarette and got to his feet. "Let's get this over with." He glanced at the phone. Should he call Cally? He'd been here since early this morning. He shook his head. Who was he kidding? She wasn't going to be worried about him. He just wanted to hear her voice. He settled his gun more firmly in the holster. He might have waited thirty-eight years to fall in love, but when he fell, he did it thoroughly. Too bad he couldn't have done it wisely.

If Dave Harcourt noticed the stern expression on his companion's face, he assumed that it was brought on by the situation with Tomás. During the drive out of the capital, few words were spoken. The radio sputtered out occasional information about Tomás's position. The government was surrounding the farmhouse, moving slowly so as to avoid warning him of their presence.

Ryder chainsmoked endlessly. His palms itched, a sure sign that trouble was on the way. There was something bothering him that he couldn't put his finger on. He kept wishing that he'd called Cally. He couldn't get the idea out of his mind. It didn't matter how many times he told himself that he was acting like a love-struck teenager.

They parked the car a mile from the farmhouse and walked the remaining distance. Several times they were stopped by soldiers and each time Harcourt explained who they were and showed his identification. Ryder said nothing, though his Spanish was considerably more fluent than his companion's.

The closer they got to the farmhouse, the stronger the feeling of impending doom became. There was something wrong. He'd lived as long as he had because he'd learned to trust his instincts. And his instincts were screaming now that something was seriously wrong.

He dropped his cigarette and ground it out with the toe of his boot. Listening to the conversation between Harcourt and a young lieutenant, it was clear that no one had seen Tomás since yesterday morning when he'd been seen outside. This morning, a car had arrived and the two men in it had disappeared into the house with a large bundle. Speculation was that they had brought either food or weapons.

It took almost twenty minutes to work their way to a front-line position where the house was visible. It was a testament to the government's fear of Tomás that they had sent so many soldiers to capture this one man. Officially, he and Harcourt were there as observers. Crouched behind a small out-cropping of rock, Ryder studied the building that was the target of all their efforts. There was nothing special about the building. Not very large, the little house showed the wear of time and climate. There was a straggly garden on one side of the house and a ramshackle chicken house in back. From where Ryder crouched, he faced the front of the building. There were remnants of narrow flowerbeds bordering a wide porch. The three stairs that led up to the porch looked sturdy if worn.

Tomás had chosen well. The house wasn't a fortress but it would cost a lot of lives if they were forced to storm it. There was no cover closer than fifty feet in any direction and there was no telling just how much weaponry Tomás had inside.

He reached for his cigarettes, letting his thoughts drift. Inevitably, he found himself thinking of Cally. She seemed to be at the end of every path his mind took these days. What were they going to do when this mess was finally wrapped up? He'd take her back to the States, of course. But then what?

His parents would like her. The thought slipped in, startling him. It had been a long time since he'd given any real thought to his family. He'd accepted that the paths he'd walked had taken him too far away to ever go home again and he rarely even thought about his childhood home. But now he found it was easy to imagine taking Cally home. His mother would immediately take her into the kitchen to find out if she could cook. Come to think of it, *he* didn't even know if she knew how to boil water. His father would bring out his good cigars and tell his son that Cally was a pretty little thing but she didn't look as if she could stand up to a New England winter—he'd have to be sure and buy a snug house for her. There was a nice salt box just down the road a piece . . .

Ryder stubbed out his cigarette, his mouth twisting. It wouldn't take long before Cally had charmed her way into their hearts just as she'd charmed her way into his. He was surprised by how badly he wanted to take her home. Maybe to show his parents that he was something more than the wolf of destruction they thought he was.

It was crazy. The only smart thing to do would be to take her back to the States and leave her with her uncle and tell her it was over. She'd be hurt but, in the long run, she'd be hurt less than if they stayed together. That would be the smart thing to do. But, if she really loved him as much as she said she did, was there any chance that they could make things work?

It was crazy but maybe, just maybe, he would take the chance. They'd take it together. He was suddenly impatient to get back to her, to hold her. For the first time in years, he was thinking about a future that held something besides his job.

Cally woke to stifling heat and a dull headache. She lay still for a long moment without opening her eyes. She was lying on something that was moving. A car. She could hear the sound of the engine. Opening her eyes, she had a moment of total panic. Black. All she could see was black. She blinked to make sure that her eyes were really open and still all she saw was darkness. Had the blow to her head blinded her? She closed her eyes, swallowing sobs of terror and forced herself to stay calm.

It was unlikely that one knock on the head was going to cause instant blindness. She moved slightly and felt relief wash over her. She was wrapped in something. She'd been too groggy to realize it at first but she was wrapped in some heavy piece of material. That was why she couldn't see. She shifted, trying to push her covering away but it didn't budge. Further exploration told her that her hands were tied behind her back and her ankles were bound together. She was rolled up like a sausage in a piece of bread and there was nothing she could do about it.

Before she could do more than consider her very limited options, the car came to a stop. Her pulse picked up, seeming to echo in the confines of her wrappings. Whoever had kidnapped her and whatever they had planned for her, now was when things would start happening.

Car doors slammed, the sound muffled. What if they were parked at the edge of a cliff and just planned to throw her off? Bound as she was, she'd be helpless. She couldn't hear the back door opening but she felt someone grab her ankles and start pulling her out. She kicked out instinctively and had the momentary satisfaction of connecting with something solid that cursed in pain. The satisfaction faded as the hands tightened around her ankles and a swift yank pulled her out of the car. Before her head could crack against the ground, another pair of hands caught her shoulders.

Cally felt like a deer being carried on a pole. Slung between her two unseen captors she was carried a short distance and then dropped roughly on a hard floor. She tasted blood as her teeth connected with her lower lip on impact.

Who had kidnapped her?

The answer came almost immediately. Someone grabbed one edge of her covering and roughly unwrapped her. Cally landed on the floor with a bump. Her eyes were dazzled by the sudden light and she blinked rapidly, trying to clear her vision.

The man who loomed above her was little more than a dark blur, rimmed with a fuzzy brilliance. She squinted, letting her pupils adjust to the light and then closed her eyes, praying that she was seeing things. But when she opened them again, he was still there, broken teeth, nasty little eyes, greasy hair and all. Tomás. She was in Tomás's hands again. It was like a recurring nightmare except that she was wide awake.

Tomás smiled, the expression full of hatred. "We meet again, señorita. Or should I call you señora now? You left so abruptly last time, you forgot to thank me for my hospitality. I'm sure you regretted that as much as I did."

"What are you going to do with me?" Her voice shook despite her best efforts.

"Exactly what I planned to do with you last time. Exchange you for something more useful. Money, escape. Perhaps revenge. Make yourself comfortable, Señora Allen. We have a few hours to wait."

He moved away, leaving her bound hand and foot, lying on the floor. She was a prisoner again. This time Tomás had even more reason to hate her.

And this time Ryder wasn't with her.

"Tomás. You are surrounded. Give yourself up." Ryder winced as the bullhorn bellowed next to his ear. He reached for his cigarettes, frowning as he noticed that there were only a few left. He was smoking too much these days. At the rate he was going, he was going to die of lung cancer long before the job killed him.

Did they really expect Tomás to just throw down his arms and walk out of the house? He lit the cigarette, narrowing his eyes against the smoke. Aside from the fact that Tomás was not the type to admit defeat, the man would be a fool to surrender, knowing what would face him as a prisoner. Execution was likely to be the kindest fate awaiting him.

It was amazing how little Tomás mattered to him at the moment. All he wanted was to get this mess over with so that he could get back to Cally. He felt years younger. He was taking a chance but it was one he felt he had to take. If disaster lay ahead, at least he would have taken the chance.

"Tomás. Give up. You have no choice."

"He's coming out." Harcourt's voice snapped Ryder out of his preoccupation and he edged his head around the rock until he could see the porch. Sure enough, the warped screen door was opening and he could see the outline of a man inside. Surely Tomás wouldn't be stupid enough to just walk out onto the porch in plain sight of all these rifles?

"I have a prisoner."

Ryder felt the hair on the back of his neck stand on end, even before Tomás stepped to the edge of the porch. The sunlight caught in Cally's hair, turning it to a white-blond beacon. Tomás held her in front of his body, making it impossible to get a shot at him without endangering her life.

Harcourt felt the man beside him tense. He'd never met the woman Tomás was holding but he knew who she was. Everyone knew who she was. Sara had told the story of Ryder's bride and, along with the description of the wedding had gone mention of her silvery gold hair.

Ryder was halfway to his feet when Harcourt's hands caught his shoulders, slamming him back to his knees. "You can't do anything by presenting yourself as a target, man." For a moment, he thought Ryder wasn't going to hear him and wondered if he could stop the man if he was really that determined. Then the muscles under his hands relaxed and he saw reason come back into the midnight-blue eyes.

"I think you all know who this is?" Even shouting, Tomás managed to gloat. He wound his hand in Cally's hair, forcing her head back. "She is the daughter of Richard Wellington who puts much money into your government. I think she should be important enough to buy passage to a friendly country for myself and my friends. Richard Wellington would not be happy if his daughter were killed. I will let you think about this."

He waited for a moment as if to be sure that they got a good look at the girl he held. Ryder's eyes covered every inch of her. She was wearing white shorts and a pale green sleeveless top. Both were dusty. Her hands were bound behind her back. Her eyes were open but it was impossible to read any expression in them at this distance. It was not impossible however to see the trickle of blood beside her mouth. Ryder was not even aware of the low groan that rumbled in his throat.

His hands knotted into fists as he watched Tomás drag her back into the house, slamming the door behind them. What must she be thinking and feeling? She was in there. Alone with Tomás and God knows how many of his men. Bound. Helpless. She couldn't even know that he was out here. And a hell of a lot of good he was doing her. It was his fault that she was in this position. He should have made her leave with her uncle. He could have insisted. Instead, he'd indulged his need to have her with him a little while longer and now she might pay for that indulgence with her life.

The minutes ticked by like hours. Now, when he was so close to losing her, Ryder realized just how much she meant to him.

He'd give her up. He made the promise to himself. If she just made it through this, he'd give her up. Never again would he put her in danger. Just by being his wife, she was a target. He had too many enemies in too many places.

His hands were shaking as he reached for a cigarette and he didn't even notice when Harcourt lit it for him. He was oblivious to the other man's look of sympathy. He dropped the cigarette, unsmoked, when Tomás called from the house. He was standing on the porch again, Cally once more held in front of him as a shield.

"You have had enough time to think about what I want. What is the answer to be, amigos?" He jabbed Cally in the ribs with the pistol he held and Ryder's fingers burned with the need to wrap them around the man's throat.

"Let the girl go, Tomás, and we will talk to you." The officer who held the bullhorn reached up to wipe a trickle of sweat from his forehead. "Let her go."

Tomás laughed, the derisive sound carrying easily on the burning hot air. "You must think I am very stupid. To leave myself without a hostage would be a foolish thing to do."

He jabbed the gun into Cally's ribs again and she winced. She was going to die. Right here on this hot afternoon in this little country, she was going to die. She felt dazed, as if she were watching everything through a fog. Her hands were numb, the circulation cut off by the ropes that circled her wrists. All day, she'd lain in the stuffy little house, listening to the plans going on around her and she'd had plenty of time to realize that she was going to die. This time, there was nothing Ryder could do to save her. For all she knew, he didn't even know she was gone.

Now, standing here, listening to Tomás talk to people she couldn't see, she wondered if Ryder would grieve when she was gone. Did he love her? He'd never said the words, though sometimes she'd been sure that she could read love in his eyes. But maybe she'd only been seeing what she wanted to see.

Tomás spoke again, interrupting her thoughts. "I tell you what. I will make a trade. I will give you the girl, if you give me the man I knew as Rico."

Cally felt as if her heart had stopped. Ryder. He wanted Ryder. Her nostrils flared. She could smell his hatred of Ryder. Tomás would kill him. His hatred was so strong that he would probably kill him, even if it meant his own death. She stiffened, trying to pull away as a man stood up from behind some rocks in front of them.

"Ryder." She barely whispered the name, feeling hope surge through her, just knowing that he was close. Hope and fear but, this time, the fear was more for him than herself. Tomás dug his fingers into her arm, drawing a whimper of pain from her.

"Hold still or I will kill him where he stands." She froze, hardly daring to breathe as Ryder stepped into the open, his hands held out from his sides, his holster visible and empty.

"Let her go, Tomás." His low voice carried easily.

"When I have you, my friend. Then you can have your little slut."

Ryder began to walk forward, his pace as easy as if he were going for a casual stroll. Cally wanted to scream at him to go back but her vocal cords seemed paralyzed. Didn't he know that Tomás would kill him? Didn't he realize that if he were dead, her own life would be worth nothing to her?

He was so close. Too close. She felt Tomás tensing and she knew, as clearly as if he'd telegraphed his intentions that he had no intention of trading her for Ryder. He was going to kill Ryder. With a sob, she went limp against him, forcing him to support her entire weight.

"Stand up!" Tomás aimed a clumsy blow at her, catching her on the temple but Cally continued to hang limply. Ryder was only a few feet away. She couldn't let him get any closer. Tomás cursed vividly, trying to stay crouched behind the protection of her body, trying to drag her upright.

She came alive suddenly, catching him completely off guard as her elbow jerked back, connecting with his groin. He cried out, releasing his hold on her for only an instant. But an instant was all she needed. She dropped flat, rolling off the edge of the porch. With her hands tied behind her back, she couldn't break the fall and she landed with enough impact to knock the wind from her.

Ryder saw the whole thing as if it happened in slow motion. Cally sagging in Tomás's hold, apparently unconscious and then suddenly coming alive. Tomás dropped her and she rolled off the edge of the porch to slam into the dirt. Tomás screamed obscenities as he brought up the gun, aiming it at Cally's helpless body. Ryder didn't even see the move with his conscious mind. There was no time to consider his options. He was only a few feet away. He launched himself toward Cally, intent on shielding her body with his.

He hit her in a rolling dive, his arms sweeping around her as he continued the roll, twisting them over and under the gap between porch and ground that he'd only been half aware of noting. He tucked her beneath him, covering her with his body as the rattle of gunfire broke out above them.

There was a burst of shots and a heavy thud above them and then complete silence. He lifted his head slowly, hardly daring to believe that he was still alive. Beneath him, Cally was utterly still. He lifted his weight from her.

"Cally? Honey? Are you all right?"

He ran his hands over her, searching for signs of injury. In the filtered light under the porch it was difficult to see much beyond the basic shape of her.

"You weigh a ton." The complaint was breathless but clear and Ryder chuckled, releasing some of the unbearable tension.

"Sorry." He lifted his weight off of her. "Let me untie your arms." She rolled to the side so that he could get at the bonds on her wrists. "Are you hurt?"

"I ruined my manicure but other than that I think I'm okay."

With Tomás dead, his supporters didn't have any interest in fighting to the death. Within minutes, the soldiers had cleared the building and Ryder and Cally were free to crawl out from under the porch. It seemed almost anticlimactic to just walk away from the scene as if nothing had happened. Cally kept reminding herself that it was really all over, that they didn't have to worry about Tomás ever again.

Dave Harcourt gave them a ride back to the city. Cally sat wedged between the two men, making polite conversation with Dave and trying not to notice that Ryder said absolutely nothing. The tension in him was almost visible. She could feel it where her shoulder pressed against his arm. She could see it in the way he chainsmoked.

They rode up the elevator in silence and she stole glances at his stern face. Was he angry with her? He'd been worried. Maybe now that she was safe, he was going to turn that worry into anger, in typical male fashion. He unlocked the door to the hotel room and Cally stepped in ahead of him.

Well she wasn't going to just sit around waiting for him to blow his top. If he planned on yelling at her, he'd find that she could yell right back. The tensions of the day hadn't all been on his side.

265

His hand closed over her shoulder, turning her to face him.

"Ryder, I—"

"Shut up."

She blinked, too stunned to even resist as he drew her closer. "What?"

"You talk too much." Cally might have argued the point but his mouth closed over hers, preventing her from speaking.

Not that she really wanted to talk. This was not a kiss like any she'd ever experienced before. The minute his mouth touched hers, she found all the built-up adrenaline and tension had a new outlet. Without a second thought, her body was molded to his, her fingers wound in his hair, pulling him closer.

There was nothing graceful about their need for each other. Fear lent a desperate edge to their desire. His hands were rough with her clothing and she heard more than one seam give. But it didn't matter. Nothing mattered except that he was touching her bare skin. She whimpered low in her throat, her head falling back as his hand cupped her breast, lifting it to receive the hungry drawing of his mouth.

She struggled with the buttons on his shirt, finally getting them open so that she could feel the hard muscles of his chest. His belt defeated her shaking fingers but his hands were there to do it for her. He lowered her to the carpet, too impatient even to lift her onto the sofa.

And there, on the floor of the living room, the

carpet rough against her back and his clothes only half off, he made love to her, drawing a response from so deep inside that Cally knew she'd never know another love like this.

Each had thought the other lost only a few hours before. This was an affirmation of life, a promise that there would be a future. The climax, when it took them, was deep and explosive, throwing them high in the air and then leaving them to float back down to earth in each other's arms.

Cally murmured a protest as he lifted himself from her, rolling to the side and collapsing on the carpet. She snuggled against his side, pillowing her head on his shoulder. He loved her. How could she ever have doubted it? She closed her eyes, letting exhaustion drift over her, feeling at peace with her world.

She might not have felt so good if she could have seen the bleak despair in Ryder's face as he stood up and lifted her into his arms to carry her into the bedroom.

"I need one ticket on the next available flight to Los Angeles."

Cally stopped in the bedroom doorway. Ryder stood across the living room, his back to her as he spoke on the phone. His voice was brisk and businesslike and she felt a twinge of unease.

She'd been alone when she woke this morning but that hadn't bothered her. After the way he'd made love to her the night before, she didn't need the reassurance of waking up with him every morning. It had bothered her a little when she realized that the suite was empty but then she'd reminded herself that there had probably been details left to deal with regarding Tomás's death.

She and Ryder needed to talk but it was almost a formality. Or so she kept telling herself. Now, fresh from her shower and wrapped in a towel, she felt a chill. Ryder must have come in while she was in the bathroom.

He turned as if sensing her presence and the eyes that skimmed over her couldn't possibly have belonged to the man who'd needed her so desperately last night. He might have been looking at someone he barely knew, not the woman he'd married.

"No, I'll only need one ticket. Issue it in the name Cally Stevens. No return."

He hung up the phone and Cally smiled at him, hoping her mouth didn't shake. Her fingers tightened on the knot that held the towel up.

"It would have been nice to be consulted about my travel arrangements."

"The last time you were consulted, you insisted on staying here and you almost got yourself killed."

"When will you be flying home?"

"I don't know."

"They must have given you some idea of how much longer they're going to keep you here."

He reached for his cigarettes, tapping the pack against his finger, his eyes on the movement. "They're not keeping me here. I'm choosing to stay."

Cally felt as if a lump of iron had settled in her chest where her heart should have been. "Why?" The question came out stark and bare, revealing all her hurt. She thought the flame of the match shook slightly but it must have been her imagination because the eyes that met hers over the cigarette were completely without expression.

"I want to stay here."

"Fine. I can deal with that. Why are you sending me home? Tomás is dead. It should be safe enough."

He shook the match out and dropped it in the ashtray before answering her question. "I don't want you to stay."

"If you're trying to hurt me, you're succeeding." She didn't try to conceal the quiver in her voice.

He stirred restlessly. "I'm not trying to hurt you, Cally. I think it's best if you go home."

"I suppose the rest of this line is that I should go home and forget about you for my own good, right?"

He studied the glowing tip of the cigarette. "Something like that."

Cally felt anger building beneath the hurt and she encouraged it, fanning it into a healthy rage. He loved her. She knew he did! Why was he being so damned stubborn about admitting it?

"And I suppose you're going to tell me that you don't love me and never did."

"I never said I loved you."

She stalked across the living room until she stood right under his nose. She was oblivious to the fact that she was a less than intimidating sight, almost a foot shorter than he was and wrapped in a bath towel.

"I've told you before and I'll tell you again, John Ryder Allen, you're a coward. Plain and simple. If you didn't love me, why did you marry me? No one held a gun to your head."

"Father Duvall suggested that you might be pregnant. I hadn't really given much thought to that before. I figured that if there was a possibility that you were carrying my kid, the least I could do was give it a name."

"Bull." He blinked at her vehemence. "If that was the case, why are you shipping me off now? I had thought of the possibility of getting pregnant and it's still there so where's all this concern about your child?"

He took a deep draw of smoke. "If you're pregnant, you'll certainly be better off in the States. You can let me know and I'll help with child support, of course."

"You've been out of the real world too long, Mr. Allen. If I'm pregnant, there's no reason to worry about child support. Hadn't you heard that abortions are legal now?" She struck hard, wanting to hurt him as much as he was hurting her. The cold façade vanished as if it had never been and white-hot rage burned in his eyes. She gasped as his hands caught her shoulders, biting into her skin.

"Don't you even think about it!"

"What does it matter to you? You don't want me. Why should you want my baby?"

Their eyes battled a moment longer before he made a visible effort to control himself. His hands dropped from her shoulders and Cally backed away, tugging the towel higher.

"You're right, of course."

"You're so damned scared of commitment that you'll throw away my love rather than risk getting hurt." He didn't look at her and Cally stopped to sniff, rubbing one hand across her nose. "Well, I'm through trying to break through your walls. You can stay there all safe and sound and never let anybody in to hurt you and you can be just as lonely as you like. I've had it."

She waited a moment, wanting him to argue, wanting him to admit that he was being a fool but he said absolutely nothing. With a stifled sob, she spun on her heel and walked back into the bedroom, slamming the door behind her.

Four hours later, David Harcourt knocked tentatively on the door and asked her if she was ready to go to the airport. Ryder was nowhere in sight and she didn't ask Dave where he was. Dave knew better than to ask questions and the ride to the airport was made in silence.

It wasn't until the plane was circling over LA that she finally allowed herself to admit that she'd lost the war. She'd fallen in love and lost. She leaned her head against the window and let the tears flow.

CHAPTER FIFTEEN

"Hey, darlin', how 'bout getting us a few beers over here?" Cally glanced up and nodded. In her opinion, they'd already had more beer than was safe but she was paid to wait tables, not give the customers advice. She gave the order to the bartender and glanced around the room. The place was less than elegant but she'd developed an affection for it.

When she'd landed here two months ago, a job as a waitress at the Log Cabin bar was the only thing available in the tiny Wyoming town. With no more money for gas, it had seemed like a reasonably good place to stop. She could have done worse.

She gathered up the beers and carried them over to the table, rejecting offers to join them with a smile and a shake of her head. Their jaws would drop if she actually did accept. She'd gained a reputation for being totally uninterested in men. Her wedding band had been noted and rumor had it that she was a recent widow. Cally was aware of the rumor and she let it sit. It kept the men from being too persistent.

Ten minutes later, she retreated to the back room for her break. Sitting on a chair with a cracked Naugahyde seat, she propped her feet on a broken stool and leaned back, closing her eyes. Fifteen minutes of peace and quiet with no one shouting for a beer and without having to dodge pool sticks on her way to deliver drinks.

Today especially, it had been hard to keep smiling. Three months. Three months to the day since she'd last seen Ryder. What was he doing now? Did he still think of her? She'd long since given up hoping that he'd come after her. If he was coming, he'd have done it long ago.

When she'd arrived in LA, she'd stayed with her aunt and uncle for only a couple of days before she began to feel as if she'd suffocate. She'd taken the cowardly way out and taken her car and the money in her checking account and just started driving, leaving them a note saying that she'd be in touch. And she had been in touch, she placated her guilty conscience. She'd called once a week, every single week.

It had been almost two months before she'd admitted to herself that part of the reason she'd run was because she was afraid Ryder might not come looking for her. It would have been unbearable to sit there, day after day, thinking that he might walk in any minute. Even worse had been the thought that he might get in touch to suggest a divorce.

She shook her head. Some people learned more slowly than others. It had taken her a long time but she was finally realizing that, whether he loved her or not, he was never going to admit it, even to himself. And if he wouldn't admit it, he might as well not love her.

With a sigh, she swung her feet to the floor and stood up. Soon she would have to go back to LA and pick up the threads of her life. Maybe there would never be someone to take Ryder's place but she had no intention of burying herself away like some pathetic heroine in a Victorian novel.

She moved over to the cracked mirror that hung at a drunken angle on one wall. The face that looked back at her was older than it had been a few months ago. Her eyes reflected the changes she felt inside. She smoothed a few stray wisps of hair back into her braid. She'd threatened to cut her hair more than once but she kept remembering how Ryder had loved to wrap his hands in it. She shook her head as she turned away from the mirror. It was going to take a while before she stopped doing things with him in mind. Amazing how he'd wound himself into her life in such a short period of time.

For the next hour, she served beer and hot dogs to her customers. She fended off suggestions, both polite and not so polite, asked after the wives of a few of the men and tried to ignore her aching feet. Weekday nights were not usually busy but tonight was an exception and it seemed like everyone and their dog had decided to stop in and have a drink or two or three.

She was leaning against the bar, giving an order to the bartender when she became aware of someone behind her—too close behind her. She turned, ready with her most freezing look and then felt her knees go slack.

"Ryder." Cally shut her eyes, sure that she was hallucinating. It was someone who looked a little like him. It was a dream and there was nobody there at all. But when she opened her eyes, he was still there.

"Hello, Cally. How are you?" The prosaic greeting seemed absurd but she answered it anyway.

"I'm fine." Her eyes skimmed over him hungrily. He looked older, more worn. The lines that bracketed his mustache had deepened. "How are you?"

"Tired." His mouth twisted in a half smile that didn't reach his eyes. "It took me a while to track you down. When you hide out, you do a thorough job of it."

"I wasn't hiding out. My money ran out here and it seemed like a good place to stay for a while." He looked oddly unfamiliar and she realized it was the first time she'd seen him in anything besides tropical-weight clothing. The sheepskin lined denim jacket added bulk to his already broad shoulders. Jeans and boots completed the outfit and all he needed was a cowboy hat and he'd fit right in with the rest of the clientele. But that wasn't really true. Ryder would stand out no matter how he was dressed.

"You gonna take this order, Cally?" The plaintive voice startled her and she dragged her eyes away from Ryder and turned to pick up the tray. Ryder didn't move and she had to edge her way around him. She carried the tray over to the table, pinning a smile on her face and hoping that none of the men were saying anything that required an answer.

What was he doing here? Had he come all this way just to ask her for a divorce? She refused to even let herself hope that it could be anything else. The wounds were still new and painful. Hoping would open herself to new hurts.

She returned to the bar, half expecting to find that he'd never been there at all. But he stood exactly where she'd left him. She set the tray down on the bar, leaning her elbow on the scarred wood and hoping that she looked calm and collected. Could he see the way her knees were shaking?

"Why are you here?" The question came out harder than she'd planned but she didn't try to soften it. There was no reason for him to know that her insides had melted just at the sight of him.

He reached into the pocket of his jacket and pulled out a battered pack of cigarettes. The movement was so familiar that she felt a stab of pain in her chest as she watched him light it.

"You shouldn't smoke. It's not good for you."

"So I've heard." He drew a lungful of smoke

and exhaled slowly, watching her through the thin veil. "I've been thinking about giving it up."

"Good." She looked away, for once wishing that someone would demand a beer. But no one was trying to catch her eye. Her eyes slid back to Ryder and she felt a spurt of anger. Did he have to be so damned good-looking? "Why are you here?"

He studied the end of his cigarette for a moment before answering. "I think we need to talk."

"I don't think so. We did all our talking in Central America."

"We're still married."

"Easily remedied."

He glanced around the bar impatiently. "We can't talk here. When do you get off?"

"We don't have anything to say to each other. Why don't you just go away, Ryder?"

"We are going to talk, Cally, whether you like it or not."

"I'm not your prisoner anymore and I don't have to talk to you if I don't want to. I'm sorry you had to go to all this trouble to find me. If you want a divorce, I'm certainly not going to argue. In fact, I'll make the trip to Las Vegas myself." She stopped, aware that her voice was taking on a strident edge. She wanted him to go away before she broke down completely. Why did he have to come here and open up all the old wounds?

He stubbed out his cigarette. "We're going to talk and we're going to do it now." There was an edge of temper in his voice.

"I really don't think we have anything to say to each other."

"Get your coat."

Her eyes widened at the command. "I'm not going anywhere with you. I have another two hours to work."

"You're leaving now."

"I am n—" The sentence ended on a gasp of surprise as his hand closed around her wrist and he pulled her away from the bar. Before she could jerk away from him, he'd lifted her and dumped her neatly over his shoulder and was striding out of the bar.

Through the rushing in her ears, she was aware of the abrupt silence that had descended over the bar. It was the only time she'd ever known anything to shut the patrons up completely. The only sound was the click of Ryder's boot heels on the hardwood floor.

Hanging upside down was not the greatest position from which to make major decisions. Cally couldn't decide whether she should be screaming, crying, trying to argue reasonably or just passively accepting her fate.

"Now just wait a minute, mister. You put her down." Ryder stopped and Cally felt the muscles in his back tense. From her position, all she could see were the toes of Don's boots. Ryder bent to set her gently on her feet, his hand clamping around her wrist before her head had stopped spinning. He turned slowly to look at the burly bartender who'd been joined by several of the patrons. Under other circumstances, Cally might have been touched by their protective attitudes. Right now, all she could see was a major brawl erupting with her right in the center of it.

"I don't remember asking you for an opinion." Ryder's tone was deadly quiet and a shiver ran up Cally's spine.

"We don't particularly like people comin' in here and haulin' off women."

"Like I said, I didn't ask you." Cally looked from Ryder to the men in front of him and it hit her suddenly that he'd take them all on. There was an aura of pent-up violence around him that frightened her but it frightened her even more to think of seeing him release that violence.

"It's all right, Don. This . . . this is my husband." At a later date, she would be amused by the way Don immediately backed down. Apparently, as long as Ryder was her husband, he was free to do as he pleased with her. Women might have come a long way but there were still places where marriage made them a man's property.

"Oh. Well, that's different."

Ryder waited a long moment to see if anyone else planned on objecting and then he turned and stepped through the door, pulling Cally with him.

She shivered, more with nerves than cold but he immediately stopped and slipped out of his jacket, draping it around her shoulders. The bulky denim all but swallowed her small figure but she didn't mind. Somewhere, deep inside, there was a tiny glow that she refused to acknowledge. He'd been ready to fight for her. Whether it was sheer bull-headedness or something more, he'd been ready to fight for her.

Without speaking, he led her to a pickup truck and opened the passenger door. She didn't get a chance to step up into the seat because his hands around her waist lifted her easily into the cab. The door shut behind her before she could say more than a murmured thank you.

It was a short drive to the lone motel that sat on the edge of town. Cally had stayed there herself during her first week here. He parked the truck and strode around to lift her down, his hand closing over her wrist again as if afraid that she was going to make a break for it. The glow flickered a little higher. Surely, he wouldn't make such a production out of this if all he wanted was to ask for a divorce?

Cally shrugged off his jacket as he flicked on the light, revealing the stark beige decor. A duffel bag sat against the foot of the bed but the bed hadn't been slept in and it was clear that he'd spent little or no time in the small room.

"I can offer you a cup of instant coffee." Funny, she could have sworn that he sounded nervous.

"No thanks." She settled herself in the one chair and waited for him to explain why he'd brought her here. She was afraid to ask questions, afraid that the answers might extinguish the last tiny bit of hope.

He turned, leaning his hip against the built-in

dresser and reaching for his cigarettes. His eyes seemed to burn everywhere they touched her.

"You're not pregnant."

"No, I'm not pregnant."

"I wondered. Your family didn't seem to know or at least they weren't telling me."

She remembered the confusing array of emotions when she'd found out she wasn't carrying his child. Relief, disappointment, depression. They'd all swirled through her.

"Why did you come?" She needed his answer now.

"Your aunt and uncle didn't know where you were. Or they weren't telling." He dropped the ruined cigarette into the ashtray and lit another one.

"I needed to get away for a while. I suppose that sounds very childish but I needed some time alone."

"Well you did a good job. It's taken me two months to track you down. I've found international spies in less time."

"International spies probably lead a more visible life than I do." Two months. He'd spent two months looking for her. Surely he wouldn't have gone to all that trouble . . . No. Don't get your hopes too high.

"Ryder, why are you here?"

Silence settled over the room. He didn't look at her and, for a moment, she thought he wasn't going to answer the question. When he did speak, it was still without looking at her.

"You know, it's a funny thing but I found out that being altruistic is the pits." He laughed without humor, his eyes at last meeting hers. "I was so sure that you'd be better off without me. Hell, I'm still sure that you'd do a lot better without me. But I guess I'm too selfish to do what I should." He turned half away, stubbing the cigarette out with enough force to crush it. "When you left, I felt like I was dying inside. I kept telling myself it was for the best, all the time I was packing like a maniac to catch the next flight to the States. I would have been right behind you but then it turned out that there were still things to be cleared up. I spent a lousy week down there before I could leave. I had reservations on every flight to LA, so that I could leave the minute they'd let me. It was two in the morning when I got to your uncle's house. He thought I was a madman."

He stopped, reaching for his cigarettes but Cally's hand stopped him. He froze, not turning to look at her, hardly even breathing.

"Ryder, why did you come looking for me?" She wanted him to say it. Just once and then she'd never ask for the words again. But this once she wanted him to say it.

His hand turned, catching her fingers in an almost convulsive grip. "I love you. Without you, my life didn't seem worth living. I know it's selfish. You're young. You've got everything ahead of you. I've got no right to tie you down. I can't offer you anything. I don't even have a job anymore. I quit and I don't know where I'm going from here.

282

There aren't that many openings for ex-spies. But . . ."

"Ryder, shut up." He turned to look at her at last, seeing the love in her eyes.

"Oh, Cally." His arms swept around her, pulling her to him, burying his face in her hair. "I love you so much."

"I love you, too."

He drew back, his fingers impatient with her hair, sweeping it loose from its braid so that he could wind it around his hands. "Every time I closed my eyes, I could see you just like this, with your hair wrapped around me and your eyes full of love. It's insane. You deserve someone who can come to you with a few illusions still intact. I can't give you . . ."

"Hush." She put her fingers against his mouth, her eyes tender. "All that really matters is that we're together. Everything else is secondary. Any problems that come up, we'll work them out."

"It may not be that simple. Cally, I haven't tried to live a normal life in almost twenty years. I don't know if I can do it."

"Ryder, you can do anything you set your mind to." She drew her fingers over the lines beside his mouth, smoothing them out. "I believe in you."

His hands slid down her back, drawing her closer, his face still serious. "You make it sound so easy but it doesn't always work that way. There's a huge gap between us, not just age but experience. No, hear me out."

Cally swallowed her objections temporarily. It

was clear that he needed to say whatever was on his mind and then she'd tell him how foolish he was being.

"I've seen things and done things that you probably can't even imagine. While you were playing with dolls, I was killing people. Sometimes I wake up in the night screaming with the memories. And that's not even the practical side of the problem.

"I don't have any training that's likely to be useful in a civilian capacity. I haven't had much to spend money on so I have quite a bit in savings but it's not enough to last a lifetime. You're still in school. You need a home, someone stable in your life. You don't need someone like me."

His voice trailed off and Cally waited a moment to be sure that he was through before she spoke.

"I'm not an idiot. I know we've got some things to be worked out. There are things in your life I'll probably never be able to fully understand but it doesn't matter. I want to be with you. I want to be your wife. I want a home with you and maybe, someday, I want to have your children. We can't wipe out the past but we can build a new future. One that has a place for each of us."

His mouth twisted. "You make it seem so simple."

"It is simple. Not easy but simple. If we love each other and we're willing to work together, we can make things work out." Her smile quivered around the edges and her eyes shimmered with tears. "Now, are you going to kiss me or am I going to have to wrestle you down and have my wicked way with you?"

His eyes lit with love and laughter, the lines smoothing out, making him look younger and happier than she'd ever seen him. "How about if I have my wicked way with you instead?"

"I don't care who does what to whom just as long as you kiss me." She slid her fingers into his hair, tugging his head downward until their lips met.

All their love and all their hopes for the future were expressed in that kiss. They might face problems but, from now on, they'd face them together. With love.